A SLAVE'S TALE

A SLAVE'S TALE

ERIK CHRISTIAN HAUGAARD

Illustrated by Leo and Diane Dillon

HOUGHTON MIFFLIN COMPANY BOSTON
The Riverside Press Cambridge

For my son,
MARK:
may he grow up
to love others,
so he may also
love himself.

PREFACE

ONCE UPON A TIME . . . with those words do all tales start, even when the storyteller does not bother to say them. For once upon a time in everyone's life the world was created, the sun rose, and the stars were fixed in the sky.

Once upon a time . . . these words were written for us, the rest we must compose ourselves. If we had only our own song to sing and no one else could understand it, we should be lonely and have no books. Our sorrows and our joys are mirrored in those of others; and therefore, we read. No man has only fair winds; and only the fool does not know that in laughter, tears are hidden.

That time of history in which *A Slave's Tale* takes place was a cruel time. The Viking era was drawing to its end, and a new society was forming. Hatred and fear walked hand in hand in Norway; and in England, and to the south, in Normandy and Brittany, the people were rising against the Norse invaders. Caught in the jaws of history, the *Munin* sailed south, ballasted only with the naïveté of its crew.

Did Helga or Hakon ever live? Did Rogen ever, like a granite whale, shoot its back out of the northern seas? I believe they did, for I have loved them; and how else should I dare to start my story, *Once upon a time* . . .

1

1

Kings, earls, and the great chieftains of Norway: all have poets who are willing to sing their praises and tell the sagas of their lives. When the eagle turns in the air and swims on the wind into the sun, man stops his work to watch with envy the ruler of the sky.

Who notices the sparrow? Yet cannot the sparrow's heart be noble, though the bird lacks the eagle's wings and the eagle's claws? Will no one ever listen to the sparrow's song, and learn from it the truth an eagle flies too high to hear?

My story shall be a plain tale: a slave's story, a sparrow's song; though much happened in my life, and I have traveled far from my native island in the north and visited countries where the sun in winter is as warm as ours is in summer.

I was born on Rogen, a small island far to the north in Norway: an island loved by the winds that come from the land of everlasting ice and snow. My mother was a slave who belonged to the chieftain of the island. His name was Olaf Sigurdson, and he was called Olaf the Lame. My mother's name was Gunhild. I was given the name of Helga, for neither dogs nor slaves can be nameless, lest their masters should not be able to call or curse them.

My father I have never known. As a little child, I used to lie in the winter nights and dream that he was a king, in some distant land. I dreamt that he would come with a fleet of ships, which had golden sails that shone like the upcoming sun. This king — my father — would free me of my bondage and make me a princess. After I had been clothed in beautiful robes, he would ask me to judge my masters. My dreams never concerned the punishment of those who had treated me harshly; not so much because I was merciful, but because I was timid. Rogen, I would let Olaf Sigurdson keep, for he had always shown me kindness, more than he had his own child, Hakon. To Hakon I would give a band of gold and the most beautiful of my father's ships.

I loved Hakon; and it was as important in my dreams to make myself worthy of being his sister as it was to gain a father who was a king. I was two months older than Hakon; and though we were not of the same blood, we were fed by the same mother's milk. Hakon's mother died in childbirth, and her son was given to my mother to be suckled. Hakon was my master, and when he grew up and became a man, he would inherit me, as he would inherit the cows that grazed on Thor's Mountain. I was his willing slave, for he never treated me as one.

Yet let no one think that he was not a boy. He led me into adventures that only a beating could get me out of. I sailed with him in his little boat, although the sea scared me; and I followed him into dark caves that even fear of my mother's stick could not have made me enter.

As I have already said, my mother was a slave; and no king or earl but only death would ever be able to free her. She had been bought by Olaf Sigurdson in Tronhjem, that summer when she was already with child. I was born when the last leaves had fallen from the trees. Sometimes the other children whispered that Olaf was my father. This pleased me, for I was very fond of him. I know now that this could not be true; and even then, I did not really believe it.

My mother was a slave. Oh, bitter is that thought that I need repeat it! She had been much mistreated as a child; and beatings — both just and unjust — had killed the human being and produced the slave. Again I repeat the word, as though it were the biggest in the world!

Measuring happiness by the stick of pain, my mother could no longer tell justice from injustice. Respecting neither herself nor her womanhood, she could not respect her child. She feared constantly that I would be in our master's way, and punished me brutally for crimes so small that they would not have caused a frown to pass over Father Olaf's face. My mother forbade me to call Olaf Sigurdson Father Olaf; and even after he told her that he did not mind, she always scowled when she heard me say it. Neither could she give real love to Hakon the Motherless, only the fawning attention of a slave. Hakon was kind to her; and being fond of her, I do not believe that he ever became aware of his own contempt for her.

On Rogen was another slave. A man named Rark, as unlike my mother as day is to night. He was a slave in name only; in spirit he was as free as Olaf Sigurdson or Harold the Bowbender, whom everyone on Rogen respected for his bravery and wisdom. Rark's way of being kind was different from Olaf Sigurdson's or Harold the Bowbender's; for they treated me kindly out of pity and he, out of love. Rark had been made a slave when he was a grown man, and he had children in a distant land. From Rark, I learned how freemen can love their children. When a freeman's child is born, something else is born with it: something invisible, frail and yet more durable than the infant. It is the love of his or her parents; and it will survive the dying child, become the ghost of the child, and haunt unmercifully the parents' hearts. I know that to Rark, I brought comfort; eased him, when his love and longing for his own children became unbearable.

Rark made me a doll when I was six winters old. He cut it out of wood and gave it clothes of skins. Rark was not a very skillful carver, but this I did not know. I gave to my rude doll all the love I dared not show to others. I had given it the name Hakon. This angered my mother, as she feared it might offend Olaf Sigurdson. After a few cuffs, I called it just "the boy." I used to hold conversations with myself, sitting quietly in the dark corner of the hall with my doll on my lap. In

6

these silent conversations, "the boy" was still named Hakon.

One day I forgot myself and started singing to the doll. A man who came from Hakon's uncle's hall laughed and said, "Olaf's wealth will ever grow; the calf of his Tronhjem cow seems already to have given him another slave." The man was a coarse drunkard, whom most men despised. He had come from Denmark, from whence he had had to flee because he had killed his brother. Yet some of the men laughed at what Sven the Dane had said, and for a moment, they all looked at me. With the instinct of the slave, I sat perfectly still with my head bent and my eyes staring at my feet.

When their laughter died away, and I was certain that the men had begun to speak of other things, I ran from the hall. This was the first time that I became really aware that I was a slave: For my child, my little boy — wooden little Hakon, with the crooked nose and the ill-proportioned body — had never in my dreams been a slave, but always an earl or a chieftain as the real Hakon would be one day. I took the doll and went to the forest, to a small clearing where I used to go when I wanted to be alone: a place so secret that I had not shown it to Hakon. With my hands, I dug a hole deep enough for my wooden child; then I buried it and placed a stone above its head. I did not cry then, but that night when Hakon asked me where my doll was I ran from the hall, out into the darkness. I hid myself behind one of the storehouses. For a long time, I heard Hakon's voice calling, "Helga! Helga!" But tears that stem from unhappiness that is past understanding, kindness cannot stop.

As is true of all slaves, most of the events in my early life were determined by the happenings in my master's. In the summer of my eleventh year, Hakon's father married Thora Magnusdaughter. One year Thora stayed with us on Rogen; and that winter I heard more laughter in the hall than I had ever heard before. But happiness frightens the slave, for he is unused to it, and believes that those who laugh in the morning will cry before the sun sets.

My master, Olaf Sigurdson, had stolen Thora from her father, Magnus Thorsen, a chieftain of great wealth who lived in Tronhjem. Thora loved Olaf Sigurdson, but her father, who had hoped to marry her to the Earl of Vigen, was determined to avenge himself against Olaf and bring Thora back to Tronhjem. So Magnus, who was old, sent his nephew, Rolf Blackbeard, with three ships and more men than there were on all of Rogen to invade our island.

There were two halls on Rogen. The main one belonged to Olaf and the other to his brother, Sigurd; but Olaf was chieftain, and Sigurd was under oath to obey him. When my master heard of the approaching fleet, he sent Hakon to bring the news of the coming danger to his uncle; but Sigurd and most of his hird remained within his hall while the invaders attacked and conquered our island. Some say that Sigurd had even helped the enemy by revealing to them where Olaf's men had hidden their flocks.

In single combat the leaders of the two armies, Olaf Sigurdson and Rolf Blackbeard, met; and each wounded the other fatally.

My master was dead! The slave's fear of tomorrow made me tremble, for Olaf the Lame had been a kind master. Some people had feared him, for they said his eyes could see the future, and that he knew the secrets of the gods. If that was true, then that knowledge was more a curse than a blessing, for Olaf Sigurdson only seldom smiled. Yet though his eyes were sad, his manners were gentle; and he judged no man but himself harshly.

Standing next to Rark, I wept at the sight of Olaf Sigurdson's dead body. I wept from sorrow and I wept from fear.

The new leader of the invaders was Ulv Erikson, called Ulv Hunger by his servants and slaves. Ulv ordered his men to steal from Olaf's hall all that was of value. The conquerors carried away what they could find: gold and silver rings; drinking horns; skins; sheep; and slaves, among them my mother, Gunhild.

From the fate of going to an unknown master in Tronhjem, Rark, my fellow slave, saved himself and me. In the confusion after the final battle, he took me to a cave deep in the Mountain of the Sun, which rises near the southern tip of Rogen. We spent many nights and days in that dark cave, and I was frightened. But one morning when Rark peeped out at the side of the boulder which blocked the entrance to our cave, he saw the ships of the conquerors sailing south; and we returned to our home.

Here new bitterness awaited us. Having been weakened by the invaders, Rogen now became prey of the most cunning and cruel of its inhabitants. Hakon's uncle, Sigurd Sigurdson, who had not raised his sword against the invaders, set himself up as ruler of Rogen. He took Olaf Sigurdson's place in the main hall; the rule of his own hall he gave to Eirik the Fox, a man who was proud of a name he should have been ashamed of.

Although all the men of Rogen knew that his father's hall was Hakon's birthright, even the bravest of them were too exhausted after their defeat to challenge Sigurd and his hird.

Sigurd sent me to the other hall, to be the slave of Eirik the Fox. Ragnhild, Eirik's wife, complained when she saw me. I was small for my age, and Ragnhild said that the work I could do would not be worth the food I ate. To do her justice, I must tell that food had never been so scarce on Rogen as it was then.

"Since she is so small, she need not eat much," Eirik argued, and scowled as he looked down at me.

If Harold the Bowbender and his sons had not lived in Eirik's hall, I am sure I should have starved that winter. From their own portions, which were not large, they gave me food when Ragnhild and Eirik were not about.

How shall I tell of that winter? It lasted long and yet I remember very little of it. I worked and I was beaten.

One thing I learned; and that is, why slaves are thought to be stupid. Life had become for me a struggle against pain, weariness and hunger. For thoughts — even for dreams — one must be able to forget one's body; and this the hungry, the weary, and those who are suffering cannot do.

The rule of a tyrant is like the reign of a storm: it destroys recklessly and ruthlessly, but it cannot last forever. By spring, even men who had at first accepted Sigurd's rule uncomplainingly grew restless and disgruntled, while Sigurd became more and more suspicious. By midsummer Hakon had to flee from the main hall, because Sigurd had made an attempt on his life. Hakon hid himself in a cave in the Mountain of the Sun, the same cave that had sheltered Rark and me from the invaders. Secretly, Harold the Bowbender collected a group of men who were willing to fight for Hakon against the tyrant.

A night of horror came like the last blast of a departing storm. When Sigurd realized how few men were willing to fight at his side, he gathered all the children and women of Rogen in the main hall; then he sent a message to Hakon threatening to kill the wives and offspring of his followers if Hakon attempted to take his father's hall.

Happily, we never discovered how dark Sigurd's heart was. The assault began before Sigurd had expected it, and it did not take long for him to decide that all was lost. Being a coward his only thought now was how to save his own life. Pale and trembling he stood among the women and children in the hall. Suddenly he grabbed me and dragged me with him through the little back door of the hall. Sigurd knew Hakon was fond of me, and thought he could use my life to bargain for his own.

We ran along the beach. Sigurd's left hand was locked around one of my wrists; and in his right he carried a sword. My heart was beating in my ears. Several times I nearly fell.

We were only a short distance from Eirik's hall when I heard someone calling Sigurd's name. Still we kept on running. Just as we reached the place where the smaller boats were moored, I stumbled. For a short distance Sigurd dragged me; then he let me go and I fell, face down, on the sand.

Our pursuer had been Rark. I saw him and Sigurd face each other. They were both panting, their mouths were wide open, and their foreheads glistened with sweat. I closed my eyes; then I heard the clashing of their swords and those desperate cries that men make — perhaps unknowingly — when they are fighting for their lives. There was a final scream; then silence. My eyes were still shut, and now I felt as if I could not open them.

A moment later I heard Hakon calling Rark's name. I opened my eyes. Sigurd was dead.

Hakon was telling me to run to Eirik's hall for help, for Rark was wounded. I trembled and started to cry. I did not know that Hakon had been victorious, that the battle was over, and that Eirik the Fox was as dead as his master, Sigurd. Still, it is to my shame that for Rark's sake I would not have gone anyway.

When Rark's wounds had been bandaged and he had fallen asleep on a bench in Eirik's hall, Hakon and I walked outside. The sun had just risen and the sky was cloudless. I looked at Hakon and thought to myself, "Now he is master of Rogen." Sadly, I added, "And I am only a slave . . . and he will never be my brother again."

Hakon looked toward the summit of Thor's Mountain, where the grave of his father was. "By Thor, by my father's memory, I promise that I shall bring back to Rogen Gunhild, who suckled me when I was born, and give her her freedom! By Odin, I swear that I shall take Rark back to his home!"

Hakon looked so brave, so like a man, and at the same time so like a child that I smiled. Then I felt his fingers in my short-cropped hair, and heard his voice.

"Let your hair grow, Helga."

Tears came into my eyes. On Rogen only the free women wore their hair long.

Here starts the tale I want to tell: for a slave is not freed by a word, any more than a man can be made a slave by the first blow of a stick.

2

"I AM NOT A SLAVE." I said the words out loud; then I looked at my bare feet and thought, "They are not a slave's feet." I heard Hakon say something, but I was not listening. I felt that the world for a moment had stopped breathing and that I was alone.

A voice cried from far away, "Hakon! Hakon!" I recognized that it was Harold the Bowbender, and the thought came to me: "He will think that I am still a slave."

Hakon took a step forward. "Let us go to my father's hall."

"Your hall, Hakon," I said.

He stared at the ground. "I am not fourteen winters old. My face cannot grow a beard."

I could only repeat, "It is your hall, Hakon."

Hakon looked at me. He was smiling; but it was that sad smile I had seen so often on his father's face; and I looked away. "Come." Hakon held out his hand to me; but I could not take it, for fear that again I should cry.

"You go. I want to stay with Rark."

Hakon started to say something; then he changed his mind. He touched my cheek gently with the tips of his fingers, turned, and walked swiftly in the direction Harold the Bowbender's voice had come from. I stood perfectly still until he disappeared behind a hillock; then I touched my cheek with my hand.

I walked towards the hall that only the day before had belonged to Eirik the Fox — that hall which after Hakon's father's death, the long year that Sigurd Sigurdson had ruled Rogen, had been my home. No, not home, for the slave cannot call his master's hall his home, any more than the captured falcon can call the wooden stick its feet are tied to, home.

Eirik's hall was not as big as the main hall, nor was it surrounded by as many or as large storehouses; yet as I stood in the yard and looked at the dragon's head which protruded from the top of the roof, a desire came over me to be mistress of it. I was only thirteen winters old; and like a child, I mistook freedom for having power over others.

It was dark inside the hall, and it took a while for my eyes to become like the owl's. Rark moaned. I walked over to the bench on which he was lying. His eyes were closed but his mouth mumbled words. I leaned over him to try to understand what he was saying in his sleep. Rark had been captured in a land far to the south of Norway. It was a strange language he was muttering in: much softer than ours; it sounded like the words one might sing to a sleeping child.

Now Rark was free, too. The thought of his leaving the island filled me with fear: who would protect me now? Rark had, I knew, both wife and children in the strange land to the south. Were they their names he was mumbling? My heart was filled with jealousy for

15

these children, whose names I did not know and whose fate might be no better than my own.

I walked over to the long table where we ate, up to the head of it, where the chieftain sat. My hands glided over the carved arms of the chair; then I sat down in it. I — the slave, the girl, the child — sat down in the seat from which Eirik had ranted and screamed at me, and promised me beatings. The drink of freedom is mixed with honey; it is sweet. My thoughts went back over all that had happened, and I rejoiced at the thought of the dead tyrants. "Good little Helga," Hakon's father had once said. Oh, he had not known me; only misunderstood meekness for goodness.

"I am glad Hakon killed you." I said the words out loud as if Eirik were still alive and could hear me. The stillness of the hall answered me and frightened me. I said again, "I am glad!"

Rark groaned and moved restlessly in his sleep. I rose and walked over to him. I put my hand on his forehead, fearing that the Wound Fever had come; but his forehead was cool. "He killed Sigurd," I thought. "Does he dream of that now?" Rark's lips parted in a smile. He was not dreaming of that, nor of the wound Sigurd had given him.

I drew the skins down over his feet, for they stuck out from under them. Rark had slave's feet like my own: brown, broad, and covered with hard skin like an animal's. Why wasn't Rark my father? Then came the thought that a man as evil as Eirik could be my father and I shivered. I belonged nowhere. Tears were already forming in my eyes when I heard the door to the hall open.

Before I had turned around, the person who had entered had closed the door again, and in the darkness I could not make out who it was. The slave's fear came back to me. I folded my hands in my lap and sat perfectly still. Moving silently along the wall towards the eastern corner of the hall was a shadow. "It is the ghost of Eirik," I thought, "come back to his home, to avenge himself." The intruder bent down and began to scratch with a knife at the earthen floor by the corner post. The noise of the knife brought back my courage: a ghost's knife cannot make a noise, nor can a ghost's hand grasp a real knife.

It was a woman. Her long hair fell down over her face. She pushed it out of the way and I recognized her, for the hair of Eirik the Fox's wife was always falling in her face.

"Ragnhild!" I called, and watched with joy her figure stiffen in fear. No, I was not "good little Helga"; but do not judge me too harshly. Much shame had my heart suffered from the tongue of Ragnhild, and much pain had my back suffered from her strong hand.

"Is it Eirik's gold you are digging for?" With surprise I listened to my own voice, feeling all the time that it was not my own but the voice of a stranger.

"Helga." Ragnhild came towards me. In her hand she still carried the knife that she had used for digging.

Rark's sword was leaning against the bench. I took it into my hands. It was heavy, but I held it out towards

17

her. Ragnhild looked at her knife and let it fall to the ground.

"Little Helga, I won't hurt you."

I kept staring at her.

"Remember . . . Remember, many times I saved you from my husband . . . Remember." She repeated the word as if it were magic, then wringing her hands, she added, "It was my husband . . . my husband."

"When did you save me?"

My words seemed to give her confidence. "Many times . . . Many times. You see, it was my husband. It was Eirik who ordered me to beat you." She looked up at me slyly. "Once he ordered me to strangle you, but I refused. I refused!"

At that moment I realized that Ragnhild, of whom I had been so frightened, was only a stupid old woman, who out of fear could tell a foolish lie. Neither Eirik nor Sigurd would ever have killed a slave; they were misers and a slave could be traded for gold. "You are lying!" I said.

Ragnhild sank to her knees. "I will share it. I will share it." Her voice was hoarse and low.

I pointed towards the door, but she did not move. "Let me keep the armband, you can keep the rest." Then as I did not answer, anger rose from that small cavern in her soul, that fear had banished it to, and she screamed, "Slave child!"

Her cry roused Rark from his sleep. With the voice of Thor, he cried out, "Who is there?"

Ragnhild ran out of the hall, leaving the door ajar.

Rark looked at me with wonder in his face: still half

18

asleep, half in the world of dreams. "Who was it, Helga?" As his forehead wrinkled, he repeated his question in a normal tone. I told him who our visitor had been, and what she had been searching for.

Rark laughed. "So Eirik had buried his gold."

"Shall I dig it up?" I asked.

"Go and fetch Hakon; but tell no one else of the gold. Gold is the heart of man: gold and greed for it."

I looked down at my hands, which still held the hilt of the sword. "I don't want gold."

"You are only a girl; and a child's heart has so many desires that there is no room for anything as lifeless as gold."

"A child's heart," I thought. "Why do grownups never understand that the world we children have within us was built by them?" I watched Rark's face intently, and then I asked out loud, "Do you want gold?"

Rark looked away from me, towards the wall as he answered, "No, not as Eirik or Sigurd did. But power, is that not another word for gold?" Turning his face towards mine again, he shouted, "Is there no man ever to be born who will want to be neither slave nor master?"

I knew Rark's question was the kind I was not expected to answer, and I felt uncomfortable under his gaze. "May I go now, and tell Hakon about the gold?"

Rark took the sword from my hands and laid it on the right side of the bench, next to his unwounded arm. "Go," he said softly; and I stood up. "Little Helga, the world is bitter, but you . . . you have a good heart."

I shook my head. As I passed the chieftain's chair on my way out of the hall, I let my hand for a moment rest on it.

3

DEATH, like the thundering waves that beat upon the rocks far beneath you, when you stand at the edge of a cliff, makes you aware of your own aliveness. Life, not golden armbands or titles, is your real treasure. When a ship is sighted during a storm, everyone will leave the warm hall to stand with wind-whipped face, staring at death. The heart beats: "I am alive!" And even the slave, his ill-clad body shivering from the cold, feels for a moment rich.

Sometimes, the ship survives the storm. The men return to smell the homey smells of the fire in the hearth. Restlessly, they walk about seeing familiar sights, touching with their hands an animal, a plow: their world which they had been so near losing. But after a few days have gone by, they will grow irritable; friends will quarrel and men shout at their wives. Unused to the calm, unused to the thought that life is long, they rebel against the weight of that treasure of which death had come so near to robbing them.

The people of Rogen were like such men. Three summers and three winters had passed since the day Hakon's father, Olaf Sigurdson, had returned from

Tronhjem with his stolen bride. Since then the storm had been ever beating on Rogen's shore. The invaders, who had come from Tronhjem to bring back Magnus Thorsen's daughter, had made many women widows. Then Sigurd Sigurdson had made himself ruler of the island, and with the help of Eirik the Fox, made hate and fear every man's companion. Hearts that have been too filled with hate are not well suited as storage places for love; and too much fear makes one shifty-eyed and suspicious.

Hakon forgave all the men that had followed Sigurd, except Sven the Dane. But for a man it is much easier to forgive than to be forgiven; forgiveness sticks in one's throat like a lump of burned porridge. Of all the men who had accepted Hakon's pardon, only Ragnvald Harelip did seem to truly repent. Ragnvald was a foolish man, filled with fear. As a child he had become accustomed to others' laughter and as an adult, to their contempt because of his fear.

For a long time, Sven the Dane was kept prisoner in one of the storehouses while Hakon and Harold the Bowbender decided his fate. Sven was a brute, an animal; and he had many crimes on his conscience, including the murder of his brother, which had caused him to flee from his native Denmark. Now was added to these crimes by the people on Rogen almost every misdeed that Eirik the Fox and Sigurd Sigurdson had committed. People stood in front of the storehouse and shouted insults at the prisoner inside. Also I felt drawn towards that building, for it was he who had taunted me about the wooden doll. I had hated and feared Sven; but to me the man inside the storehouse was not my enemy and that is why no curses came to my lips. All this was not clear to me then, for they were not thoughts but feelings that I could not have formed into words.

Once when I stood among a group of women staring at the locked door, Ragnhild, Eirik the Fox's wife, came. She screamed at Sven, "Murderer!"

I bowed my head, ashamed of being there. The other women took up her cry. I looked up and saw that Ragnhild was staring at me. I had not spoken to her since that day I had prevented her from digging up her husband's treasure.

"It was all his fault." Ragnhild moved closer to me as she spoke. Instinctively, I took a step backward. "He got my husband to do it all: he and Sigurd Sigurdson." She was waiting for me to agree, as if that should make peace between us; but I looked away.

"He has a slave's soul!" At the word "slave," I stepped back; but my gaze again met hers. Now it was Ragnhild who looked down at the ground; and for what seemed a long time, both of us were silent.

"There are more slaves than freemen on Rogen," I thought; but my tongue refused to let the words pass my lips. Just at that moment when the silence became as hard to bear as blows, Ragnhild turned and walked away. The other women followed her. There was even a girl of my own age among them: Rigmor, Ragnvald Harelip's daughter. She, too, looked at me with contempt. I followed them with my eyes, while I thought,

24

"Now, Helga . . . Now you have enemies."

I walked down to the longship that lay drawn up upon the beach. Sitting in its shade, my hands playing with the sand, I thought about Sven and Ragnhild. When I was a slave, both Sven and Ragnhild had often mistreated me; but they had not hated me, any more than they hated the cow, to whom they would give a blow when it did not stand still at milking time. The first harvest of my freedom was hate; yet the thought made me happy and I smiled.

"What are you laughing at?" Hakon was standing beside me.

"I wasn't laughing, I was only smiling."

Hakon threw himself down beside me. "And what makes you smile?"

I did not want to tell him, so instead of answering I said, "What will happen to Sven the Dane, Hakon?"

Hakon took a pebble and threw it towards the sea. It fell among the wet stones along the shore. "Harold wants me to have Sven the Dane killed."

Ragnhild's cry, "Murderer!" echoed in my ears while I said, "And what do you want to do?"

Hakon's hand grabbed another pebble. "He hasn't deserved any better." This time, the pebble reached the water.

"No . . ." I was thinking of Ragnhild and all the others on the island, who so short a time ago would have rejoiced at Hakon's death.

"Harold says it is necessary." Hakon, who until now had kept his gaze out over the sea, turned his face towards me. "I don't want anybody killed," he said.

It struck me with surprise that Hakon's face was no longer that of a thirteen-year-old boy, but that of a man. I looked down at the sand and wondered if I, too, had changed, and if my face were a woman's. "Pardon him," I said.

"I can't!" he cried. "Little Helga, you are too good."

"Too good," I thought. "Why is it we cannot understand each other?" It was not because I was too good that I wanted to spare Sven, but because I was frightened. "From tyrant's blood strange flowers grow," I said aloud. They were lines from a poem I had once heard. I spoke them now as they came to my lips, like a ghost from nowhere.

Hakon rose; his hand glided along the side of the ship. "I shall banish him from the island." I nodded in agreement. Hakon sighed and said, "There is so much to do."

Timidly, I finally asked him, "Was there much gold in Eirik's treasure?"

Hakon shrugged his shoulders; then when he saw that I was unhappy, he smiled. "We need so much on Rogen. The sword is a poor plow, and I do want to keep my word to Rark and take him home. There was gold enough so that we can buy a sail in Tronhjem." He nodded towards the boat. "But not much more than that."

I was terribly disappointed, for I had hoped that Eirik's treasure would solve all the problems gold knew the answer to.

"It was well, though, that Ragnhild did not get a chance to dig it up."

I smiled my thanks for Hakon's words. "And I am glad you are only banishing Sven."

But Sven was not to be banished; he was forever to rest on Rogen, and yet Hakon was to be spared passing sentence on him.

A few days later, a meeting of the people of Rogen was called to determine Sven's fate. It was held in the yard in front of the main hall. The chieftain's chair had been taken outside and placed there. At Hakon's heart side stood Harold the Bowbender and next to him, his sons; on the other side was Rark. The rest of the men took their places, making a circle; behind them were the women. I stood behind Magnus the Fair. The summer sun had bleached his hair almost white.

Two men half carried, half dragged Sven the Dane into the middle of the yard, while the people shouted and cursed. Magnus the Fair did not shout, but mumbled, "When swine are hungry, they grunt." Magnus' words hit me like a blow from an open hand, for I, too, had wanted to scream like the others. I took a few steps backward, but soon curiosity directed my feet forward again.

Sven's hands were tied behind his back; his face and clothes were dirty; his hair and beard unkept. He looked like a frightened animal, not like a man. His eyes moved restlessly round the circle. When his glance fell on those who had been his companions when he had stood high in Sigurd Sigurdson's hird, one or two turned away, but most shouted even louder than before.

"Sven, you have been accused of murdering Eigil Grimson and Thorkild Olafson."

Sven did not answer but looked at the ground.

"Are you guilty?" Again I heard Hakon's voice and wondered that my childhood playmate was chieftain of Rogen.

"I didn't!" Sven's words sounded like a cry.

Harold the Bowbender's face, that had so much kindness mixed with its sternness, was disfigured by a malicious smile. I remembered that Eigil Grimson had been the same age as Harold, and Harold's closest friend. Eigil and Thorkild had disappeared two days after Sigurd Sigurdson had proclaimed himself ruler of Rogen. Sigurd had said that they had been drowned while fishing; but few had believed him, for everyone knew that they had been friends of Hakon's father and bitter enemies of Sigurd.

"It was Eirik the Fox who did it." Sven's voice was thin and pitiable.

"Liar!" cried Harold; and the men took up the word and made a song out of it. "Liar. Liar. Liar!"

In my excitement, I did not realize how near I had stepped to Magnus. When he turned around, he almost stumbled over my foot. "You, too, Helga?" Magnus the Fair's face was so close to mine that I could feel his breath. "In the old times, they used to drink their enemies' blood. Would you like some, Helga?"

I drew up both my hands and covered my eyes.

28

"Well, you have more reason to hate him than all the rest have." For a moment, Magnus' hand rested on top of my head; then he turned and walked away.

I wanted to run after him and tell him that I did not wish Sven's death, but my feet would not move.

A shout of disgust from the people made me turn my eyes again towards the spectacle. Sven had fallen on his knees and was begging for mercy. The tear-streamed face makes us turn away and harden our hearts, for we fear that it is our own face we are seeing.

Sven was crawling on his knees towards Hakon's chair and repeating, over and over, his name: "Hakon Olafson . . . Hakon Olafson . . ."

Hakon's face was white, and his hands grasped the arms of the chair.

Suddenly, Ragnvald Harelip stepped out of the circle, and with spear in hand, ran towards the helpless Sven. He thrust the spear through Sven's back. When Sven fell, he screamed; and in the silence that followed, the scream still seemed to linger in the air. No one moved except Ketil Ragnvaldson, who with drawn sword leaped to his father's side to protect him. But it was not necessary; no one wanted to touch Ragnvald.

Sven was dead. Erp the Traveler kneeled at his side and examined the wound. Hakon could not speak. He swallowed a few times, then shook his head. Harold the Bowbender stepped forward and ordered two of the men to carry Sven's body back to the storehouse, and told Ketil to take his father into the hall.

I watched Ketil and Ragnvald enter the hall, and Hakon rise from his chair. The people walked away silently, as if no one could bear the sight of his neighbor's face. I kept standing where I was, fearing that if I tried to move I would be sick.

Finally, when I was alone, I walked to the place where Sven had been killed. At the sight of the blood I turned and started to run. Leaning against a low wall, I vomited and cried at the same time. From behind the wall, I heard the low grunt of the pigs. I remembered the words of Magnus the Fair, and thought, "The swine have been fed now."

4

"THERE IS NO MAN on Rogen who would not have killed Sven." It was Harold the Bowbender, talking with Rark and Hakon at the end of the big table in the hall, two weeks after Sven's death. I was sitting in the shadows by the wall, trying to sew a pair of shoes.

"With his hands tied? That does not speak well of the people of Rogen." Though Rark's voice seemed calm, I could hear that he was suppressing anger.

"Ragnvald Harelip is a fool," Harold commented, in the same tone he would use for describing the weather.

"It was murder." Hakon's voice had the same undertone as Rark's. One could hear in the way all three of them spoke that this was something they had discussed often.

"If Ragnvald had not killed him, what would you have done with him?" When Hakon didn't answer, Harold the Bowbender continued, "Ragnvald Harelip's foolishness was a gift to the wise. Sven is buried and a lot of crimes are buried with him. Let them all rest, and let Loki's wife take his soul, if he had one." Harold rose, looked at his companions who remained silent, nodded and left the hall.

31

"Harold is right . . ." Hakon shook his head. "And somehow, he is all wrong."

I could not see Rark's face, yet I was sure that he was smiling. "The justice of earth and the justice of heaven; and not often are they one."

At Rark's words, I started thinking of his gods: that strange god who with the help of his son ruled the people in the south. Harold the Bowbender was like Thor. Was Rark the image of his god? I pricked my finger with the needle. It hurt, for it was the big, clumsy needle used for the sewing of skins. I put my finger in my mouth to suck the blood; and I felt a little afraid while doing it, for my mother had always hit my hands when I sucked my fingers.

"When the gods, the Fenris Wolf, the Midgard Worm, and all the giants who live in the mountains of fog and ice are dead, then Balder will come and rule the world; and then, no man shall carry a sword." Hakon was repeating the old words, the words that many women have moaned over the dead body of a son or a husband.

"Balder." Rark spoke the name with contempt. "Balder was killed by Loki, and Loki is one of your gods."

For a moment, both of them were silent; then Rark rose. "Harold is right, Hakon." He picked up the fishing lines, on which he had been knotting hooks. "No one has so broad shoulders that he can stop the sun from moving," he said and sighed. Then he, too, departed from the hall.

Hakon and I were alone now, and I watched him as he sat frowning at the end of the table. "Do you agree with them, Helga?"

I did not know that Hakon had noticed me. "I was not listening." I lied because I had found his question so difficult to answer.

When Hakon thought very deeply, he had the habit of running his fingers through his hair. Watching him comb his hair with his hands, I said, "Maybe there are two kinds of justice."

Hakon laughed. "Remember, you weren't listening."

I blushed and felt my cheeks grow warm. Taking up my sewing again I mumbled, "There are two kinds of sun . . . The pale one of night, which we call the moon; and the blazing one of day. Is there a pale justice, too . . . one of shadows and darkness? If there is, then that was the justice that guided Ragnvald's spear."

Hakon was silent for a moment; then he shook his head gently. "At night Thor's Mountain looks bigger than it does in daylight; but it is our eyes that night dims, not the size of the mountain."

"Are you going south in the spring?" While I waited for Hakon's answer the world held on to me with so firm a grasp that it hurt.

"When the snow of next winter melts on Thor's Mountain, then we shall sail: first to Tronhjem to buy a new sail and trade wool for fox skins, to sell in the south."

"Will you take me with you, Hakon?" Hakon said

33

nothing; but in his silence, I heard his answer. "I am afraid to stay here alone." I had stopped working on my shoe and my hands rested in my lap.

"Harold the Bowbender will rule Rogen while I am gone, you have nothing to fear."

How could I explain my fear to Hakon so that he would understand me, when I did not understand it myself? Harold would take good care of me, he would allow no harm to come to me: I knew all the arguments that Hakon could use against me. I bent my head.

"Do you think that Harold would allow anyone to harm my Helga?"

At the words "my Helga," I smiled; and Hakon, taking my smile for agreement, stood up. "You are my sister."

He touched my hair and tears formed in my eyes and rolled down my cheeks. That was what I had always wanted, for Hakon to be my brother; and now his saying that he was, only made me feel sad.

"One summer only, we shall be away; then when the short, fall days come again, I shall be back. What shall I bring you from Rark's homeland?"

I did not reply and I was thankful that the twilight of the hall kept my tears from being seen.

"A gold comb or an armband so heavy that it would be worth ten men's lives?"

An armband so heavy that it would buy ten slaves? No, I did not want that. Still, I said nothing.

"Helga, the best that I can bring back will be yours."

Again I blushed; for I had thought silently, "Come back yourself, Hakon, and that will be my gift."

"What are you making?" Hakon asked, and took the shoe from my hand.

I was making a shoe from the skin of a sheep. It was the first pair I had ever tried to make. They would keep me warm when winter came.

"I shall get you shoes like those the princesses wear in the south."

"Yes, that I should like better than gold rings."

Hakon laughed at my eager tone. Suddenly the door to the hall opened. It was Ketil Ragnvaldson who had come to fetch Hakon. For a moment the room was flooded with light.

When the door closed behind them, I put away my sewing and stretched out upon the bench. As I lay there, staring at the wooden walls, thoughts from my childhood came back to me. The veins in the wood were faces, the knots were eyes staring at me. When I had been very young, I used to draw the covers over my eyes to shut out the faces. In the warm darkness, feeling safe and courageous, I would decide my dreams for the night. I would tell myself I was a princess; and my mother, Gunhild, would come to me, kneel in front of me, and tell the sad tale of how she had stolen me from my real mother's bed. I would then forgive Gunhild for her evil deed. Not long after, I would pass into the land of sleep and real dreams. It was not always I could direct my dreams; sleep sometimes unmade the princess and brought back the slave. I would wake

sweating and shivering. When I threw back the skins, the dim light from the fire which burned in the middle of the hall would seem friendly and kind.

That afternoon, the faces in the wall would not appear. The knots would not become eyes, nor the veins a monster's features. This made me content and proud. I whispered, "Never . . . Never again shall you scare me. Never!" I remembered a verse that I had often heard Hakon's father speak:

> Dreams make young the old,
> Warm the blood that is cold,
> Whisper in the brave men's ears
> The terror of forgotten fears.

My mind was wandering, leaping from one thing to

another, as sleep closed my eyes. I thought of Olaf the
Lame, Hakon's father; and his face appeared in front of
me, so close that I might have touched it, had I held out
my hand. The features of his face changed and they
became my mother Gunhild's. She spoke to me, but her
voice was Father Olaf's, "Take care of my son!"

I woke. Startled, I closed my eyes again; but dream
and sleep were gone. I sat up on the bench and folded
my legs beneath me; then putting my elbows on my
knees and my face in my hands, I thought of my
dream: was it a warning? Didn't the gods speak to men
in their dreams, for where else could dreams come
from? But why had Father Olaf worn the face of my
mother? Ulv Erikson had taken my mother to Tronhjem as part of his booty. Was my mother dead? Was
I now as much an orphan as Hakon? I put my hands in
front of my eyes, as if I were going to cry; but no tears
came.

"I will not stay behind. I will sail with you, Hakon!"
It gave me courage to speak the words out loud.

A strange inhuman cry came from the darkest corner
of the hall. Fear held my breath until I realized that it
was only the cry of Freya the Old. Freya was always
getting warnings in her dreams; and some people said
that if half of her prophesies came true, not a man
would be alive on Rogen.

"I will sail with Hakon to Rark's country. Give me
omens for the trip, Freya." I could not see her, but I
heard her moving towards me in the darkness.

"The strongest sails will rip. All ships can death out-
strip."

My hands knotted themselves in anger, I hated that old woman and her omens. "Those are verses from the Saga of Sigmund the Strong. Any child knows them," I said angrily.

The old hag laughed; but she said no more, and I felt comforted in having had the last word. I remembered the way Magnus the Fair had described Freya the Old: "When the path of wisdom and age parts, it shall never join again."

As I picked up my shoe and started sewing once more, I said to myself, "I shall sail with Hakon!"

5

THE WINTER that year had a stern face, and Hakon was not to sail the following spring. Too much work remained to be done on Rogen for so many of the men to leave the island for so long a time. Erp the Traveler, who was famed as a steersman, said that few had been lucky enough to travel so far and return during one summer.

Rark was very disappointed, for he had hoped to see his home that summer. So were most of the younger men, who all had more taste for adventure than for work in the fields.

If the winter was unkind, then the summer seemed to want to undo the damage the winter had caused. Only one lamb died during the lambing season. Grass was plentiful; great stacks of hay were piled up around the hall, promising more than enough food for the cattle next winter. There were even more herring and cod caught that summer than most years. The people took the rich harvest as an omen that the gods looked with pleasure once more on Rogen. Many of them began to talk of Hakon's luck, and look with admiration upon their young chieftain.

As Hakon's sun ascended into the sky, its rays fell on

his favorites. Harold the Bowbender was now the most respected man on Rogen, second only to Hakon. That Rark had once been a slave was almost forgotten, for he had killed Sigurd Sigurdson in single combat. Also I felt the difference: I slept nearer the fire, and at night my body was covered with a quilt of down. The quilt had belonged to Hakon's mother and had kept Thora Magnusdaughter warm the winter she lived among us. But it gave me many enemies, for as the chieftain's seat at the end of the table was the symbol of Hakon's power, my nightly covering was a symbol of my favor with Hakon.

Most of the women were happy that the men could not leave that summer, for few like to see their husbands or sons sail away in Viking. Many a ship has never returned, and many that have come back have brought to a wife or mother only the tale of her husband's or her son's death.

Although the sun warms man, it is not a friend in the same way that the fire on the hearth is. Hakon was now chief of Rogen; and though I was no longer a slave, the difference between our positions seemed greater than ever. Seldom did I get a chance to talk with Hakon alone, for there were always men about him. I grew sullen as I found that my freedom made me more lonesome. I was growing up. I was neither child nor woman, neither free nor slave; ever living in spring weather, when winter and summer can be felt on the same day.

I learned to shoot with bow and arrow; mostly in the vain hope that my skill should change Hakon's mind, and I would be allowed to sail south with him. I noticed that summer, that my body was changing and sometimes I felt that it was something separate from myself. I had begun to think differently, too: I, who as a child would cry at the sight of a lame bird, could now with my arrows kill a hare and rejoice at my hunter's luck. I liked being outside, and no longer feared the night, but would walk alone when the winds were asleep and the full moon had changed all the trees and shrubs to silver.

My enemies were among the women. I believe they felt it an insult to have to sit at table with me, a former slave. Especially Signe, the widow of Sigurd Sigurdson, and Ragnhild, Eirik the Fox's widow, hated me; but because of their husbands' crimes they had little power. Yet I feared that when Hakon was not there to protect me, they would show their hatred more openly.

When the first fall storms came, and the cattle were brought down from the mountains and the sheep brought home from Grass Island, the men started to talk of the voyage. I listened to the young men's heroic dreams. The lands beyond the sea drew our thoughts as the currents in the sea draw the ships. Hakon spoke of the trip as a trading voyage, and he talked little of his real reason for taking it. I think he feared that some of the men might think it foolish to sail so far for the sake of a man who had once been a slave. Rark rarely spoke of the trip; but many times that winter, I saw him stop his work and stare out in front of him as if the walls of the hall weren't there.

Only once during that winter did I talk to Hakon of

41

my wish to sail with him; that was when I discovered that four of the women of Rogen would be part of the crew. Hakon would not even listen to my arguments. The next day I spoke to Rark. Rark told me that in the south, women never went on sailing trips, nor did they shoot with bow and arrow or carry a sword. Rark already seemed to be living more in the south than he did with us.

Finally, I decided that I would hide on the ship before it sailed, knowing that once the ship had been at sea more than a day, Hakon could not give an order to return to Rogen just to bring me back. My decision gave me comfort at night, when all things seem possible; but in the mornings when I woke, I feared that my plan was foolish and childish.

When the Midwinter Feast was well past, and I was fifteen winters old, I looked for the signs of spring with dread. Each morning the sun rose higher above the sea; and I knew that one morning the winds would come from the south and the snow would start to melt.

6

DRIP . . . DRIP . . . DRIP . . . I could hear the melted snow running off the roof. It was late in the evening, but only the children were asleep. The men were restless and sat in groups talking to each other. I pulled the cover up over my ears, but I could still hear the dripping from the roof. It was as if each drop said, "Spring . . . spring . . . spring . . ." I threw off my quilt and sat up upon the bench. Near me a mother was singing. I strained my ears to pick up the words of her song, which she chanted low to the already sleeping child.

"Dream, my child,
Close your eyes,
Sleep a while
The sun will rise.
Spring has come,
Winter is gone.
The snow is melting
On the roof.
Sleep my flower,
Sleep my bird,
Soon the grass

Will grow.
Green the mountains,
Green the fields,
Blue the summer sea.
Dream, my child,
Close your eyes,
Sleep a while,
The sun will rise."

I knew the song, though my mother had never sung it to me. She used to sing it to Hakon when he could not sleep. The thought that I did not even have the memory of having once been sung to by my mother made me feel so poor; and then, so angry.

Hakon was sitting at the end of the table, talking to Harold the Bowbender. They were too far away for me to hear what they were saying, but I was sure they were talking about the voyage. I felt cheated, angry, and filled with self-pity.

I lay down again upon the bench, and pulled the quilt over my head. I mumbled aloud, "May Loki burn the ship! May Thor split its mast and Father Odin spread its ashes!" Having uttered the curse, I became frightened; tears were in my eyes. "I didn't mean it, Father Odin . . . Hear me . . . I didn't mean it."

What if the gods had heard my curse, but not my plea? Quietly I rose from the bench, dressed myself, and went outside. It was a clear night, and there was a half-moon. The snow was soft and wet under my feet.

"Your shoes will be soaked." Saying something so ordinary gave me comfort. I was walking towards the little grove that was sacred to Odin; in the middle of it was a clearing.

Rark and Thora Magnusdaughter always spoke to their god on their knees. It was not customary to speak to Odin in that position, but my feeling of shame made it natural for me to kneel.

"Odin, Father of all things, hear me, Helga . . ." I paused and then added to humble myself, "The slave child." The wind sighed in the trees and an owl hooted far away. The snow was moist and cold against my bare knees. Stumbling over the words, I made my prayer. "Protect Hakon, Rark, and the men who sail with them. Let no harm come to them. I am a foolish girl. Do not listen to the words I spoke in the hall . . . Keep Loki away from their ship."

I stood up and glanced towards the sky; a tiny cloud passed by the moon. "And let me be in the ship when they sail!" I begged. An owl hooted three times and I felt sure that it was a good omen.

When I had reached the edge of the clearing, I leaned up against a birch tree and looked back. In the silence I could hear the water dripping from the branches of the trees. "The song of spring," I thought, "and it no longer makes me feel sad." From the other side, a fox entered the clearing, sniffed the air, and stood still. It was thin, mangy and beetle-starved. How long had it been since it had eaten enough to fill its stomach? I felt so sorry for the fox, I wanted to speak to it: tell it that spring soon would be here, when rabbits and mice would come out of hiding. But as suddenly as it appeared, it was gone.

Someone was walking through the snow towards the clearing. "It is Hakon," I thought. So certain was I that my guess was right that I smiled as I hid behind the tree. I intended to frighten him.

It was not Hakon. It was Signe, the widow of Sigurd Sigurdson. She looked around the clearing many times. When at last she seemed satisfied that she was alone, she walked towards the stone in the center of the clearing, which was used for offerings. In one of her hands, she held a knife; in the other, she clutched by its feet a hen. She held the knife and the hen up towards the moon; lowered them and held them up again. Seven times she did this, raising and bending her head in time with the movements of her arms. Then with the knife she cut off the head of the hen. Dripping the blood onto the stone, she spoke to Odin. In the still night, the words sounded loud and clear.

"Odin, Father of all, revenge my husband, who was killed by a slave." She held up the dead hen. (I trembled, thinking of Rark who had killed her evil husband.) Now she placed the hen on the stone, and her hands rose towards the moon, as if she were going to pluck it from the heavens.

> "Anger the sea
> Drown them all,
> Let none return
> Alive in fall."

Signe looked about herself once more; then she cut off the legs of the hen. She threw one in front of her, and the other back, over her shoulder, while she spoke.

"Run east. Run west. Go to the Giants' hall and tell them Signe calls. Wake the Fenris Wolf, the Midgard Worm, and tell Loki of Hakon Olafson's crimes."

She spoke no more; but bowed in the four directions of the winds before she walked away, back towards the hall, leaving the hen on the stones and its feet — far from each other — lying in the snow.

I stood staring at the stone, expecting Odin himself to carry away the offering. A cloud drifted past the moon and hid its face. The trees grew dark around me. I had given nothing to Odin. Silently, I prayed to him, telling him that I was poor, that I had no chickens I could offer to him. In the midst of my prayer, I thought, "Where did Signe get that hen from?" She had no hens of her own. It must have been stolen from Hakon's roost.

"A stolen hen, Odin . . . How can a god eat a stolen hen!" As I uttered these words, the cloud left the moon's face. Again the clearing was covered with silver. I looked at the offering stone.

The fox had come back. It had its front paws up on the stone and was stretching its neck to reach the hen. "Never would Odin come in the skin of a fox," I thought, "but Loki could." I held my breath. With a push of its hind legs, the fox was up on top of the stone; its jaws round the dead bird. The fox forgot fear and tore the neck off the hen; while it stood there, the fox was a perfect target in the clear night.

"The gods are hungry." I had spoken aloud. Away was the fox, and away was the hen. I started to laugh;

but the awe I held for the holy place and the silence soon stopped my laughter.

I walked over and picked up the hen's feet. I put them on top of the offering stone. Then the idea of asking help from Rark's god came to me.

"God of Rark, God of the men of the south, help Hakon . . . and help me."

Again I had fallen on my knees. When I got up, I realized that my feet were numb with cold. I ran towards the hall, saying under my breath, over and over again, "It was only a hungry fox . . . only a hungry fox."

7

CURSE THOR'S BROKEN HAMMER!" Magnus exclaimed.

All morning Magnus the Fair and I had been working alone on the longship. I placed the tar-filled oakum along the seams, and with his mallet, Magnus drove it in between the boards. Magnus now looked with disgust at his broken mallet. His face appeared to me so funny that I could not help laughing. For a moment I feared that he would throw the mallet at me; but he threw it to the ground and started laughing himself.

"The ship is bewitched. We shall never sail unless we offer a girl with a pure heart to Odin."

I stopped laughing; but catching sight of the laughter still lurking in his eyes, I said, "What is a girl? A piece of driftwood too short to make an oar. No, it is not enough to satisfy Odin. You had better offer a boy, or a man . . . a full-grown man with golden hair and—"

Magnus had thrown a big wad of dried seaweed at me. He had missed. I picked up the seaweed and aimed it at his face. I did not wait to see whether it had hit the mark, but ran around the ship. When I reached midship, I stopped to see from which end of the ship Magnus would come.

The world was still except for the cry of the gulls on Grass Island. On tiptoe I walked towards the bow of the ship. I thought that Magnus might be angry, and I wanted to call out loud, "I'm sorry, Magnus." But I said nothing. At last, curiosity made me stick my head around the bow. Magnus grabbed one of my ears and with a scream of triumph dragged me around the bow.

"I have got the witch. Oh, Odin, hear me! I, Magnus, have caught Loki's little sister!"

I kicked Magnus across the shins. He lifted me up by my shoulders and threw me down upon the beach. Kneeling, he pressed my shoulders into the sand. I turned my head and bit his wrist. He cried out as if I had bitten him hard.

"Odin, she has poisoned me! Her fangs which carry the poison of the Midgard Worm shall be my death." His hand rose as though he were going to hit me; still, I laughed at him. He touched my hair and his face grew wonderfully sad, as if I had really hurt him. Only for a moment did his hand rest on my head; then he jumped up and returned to his work. I lay still in the sand feeling sad and filled with joy.

The sun was almost summer warm. Lazily, I watched Magnus. He had taken a smaller mallet. He hit the little stick of iron, with which he was driving in the oakum, so hard that I feared it might go through the heavy board.

Drawn up on the land, the boat looked so huge. I counted the holes: on one side there were fourteen and the same on the other. Magnus had told of ships in Tronhjem that had twenty-five oar holes on either side.

I tried to imagine one of them and decided that it must be a king's ship.

Our longship was named *Munin*, and Hakon's father had bought it in Tronhjem. Above me in the spring air a gull was riding on the soft summer breeze; it was hardly using its wings. Father Odin's ravens: were they real birds, or were they witches he had turned into birds? They were called Hugin and Munin; and it was after one of them our ship was named. They flew to all corners of the earth and returned to whisper in Odin's ears all the things they had seen on their journey. "What could a bird see that was worth telling?" I thought.

Magnus the Fair had stopped hammering, and had thrown down the little mallet. He stood with the larger one in his hand, contemplating its broken handle.

"I am going to put a new handle on it."

I nodded but did not get up. He seemed about to say something more, but then he turned and walked up towards the hall.

It would not be many days more before the men would leave; and I had yet to make a real plan for smuggling myself on board. I rose, brushed the sand from my legs, and walked to the bow of the ship. *Munin* did not have a dragon's head, but on the heavy timber that formed its bow were carved figures of the fishes of the sea. The bow became slimmer and slimmer, until far above the deck it ended in a curled dragon's tail. I had to lean my head back to see it, for it was three times as tall as I was.

Walking beside the ship, I let my hand run along its

boards. When I came to midship, I stopped. There the railing was not high. Reaching up, I was able to grab hold of it and lift myself until I could rest my elbows on it; then, swinging my body, I managed to get one foot in an oar hole. I pushed with my foot and slid over the railing. Headfirst, I tumbled into the boat.

The loose boards of the deck had been removed, for they were in the way while the ship was being repaired. I had fallen to the very bottom of the ship and hit my head against one of the heavy wooden beams that supported the deck. "Wood to wood," I whispered and giggled, for that day my good humor was as impregnable as Valhalla, Odin's hall.

I peered through one of the oar holes, up towards the hall; but I saw no one. The ship smelled pleasantly of tar. I sat down upon the mast board (the only part of the deck that could not be removed from the ship). It was heavier than the boards of the rest of the deck, and there was a hole in it, through which the mast was passed, down into the mast-fish. The mast-fish is a heavy block of wood shaped a little like a fish; it anchors the mast to the keel.

Underneath the deck would be stored the food, weapons, and the skins that Hakon hoped to sell with profit in Rark's land. Would there be room there for me to hide? I sat down on the keel, aft of the mast-fish. The top of my head could just pass under the oak pieces which supported the deck. "But this will be the first place loaded," I said aloud. I walked farther aft, until the ship was no wider than I was tall. I lay down and found that even here there would be room enough for me, though certainly it would be more comfortable to lie midship.

"Helga!"

I knew it was Magnus calling me, but I did not answer; instead I climbed towards the bow of the ship as silently as I could. At the foremost of the oar holes, I stopped and looked out. Magnus was standing right beneath me, looking so bewildered that I almost laughed. Next to the keel board, I found some little stones among the sand that was lodged there. I put a pebble in my mouth and blew it at him, through the oar hole. He was standing with his back towards me, and the pebble hit him on the neck.

As I heard Magnus scream, "Witch!" I ran towards midship. I meant to hide again; but suddenly for no apparent reason I decided against it, and jumped over the side. I landed on my feet, for which I was very grateful, because in my new mood I was a grownup, and falling on my face would not have pleased me.

"Did you fix it?"

For answer, Magnus held up the mallet with its new handle for me to see. I grabbed some of the tar-filled wool and cow's hair, and started pressing it along the seams of the boards. Soon I heard Magnus hammering again. We worked silently for a while. My hands were all black from tar; and though this had never bothered me before, suddenly it made me angry.

"The princess with the tar hands," I whispered and started making up a story about a king's daughter who was very beautiful but whose hands were black as tar. I usually had no trouble making up stories, but I could not find any reason why the princess should have such dirty hands. "Because she was a frightful pig!" I said aloud and laughed.

"What did you say, Helga?" Magnus stopped hammering and turned towards me.

I blushed and stammered, "When . . . When is the boat going into the water?"

"Hakon hopes tomorrow. It has to lie and soak for at least ten days." Magnus put down his hammer and walked towards me.

I kept on working, as I had nothing more to say. Though my back was to him, I was aware that Magnus had sat down on the sand behind me.

"Helga?" I did not turn my head, nor did I answer him. "Helga!"

Leaning against the side of the boat, I looked down at him. He was scooping sand up with one hand, and letting it run down into the other.

"Helga, how many winters old are you?"

"Fifteen," I whispered.

"I am twenty-two."

I wrung my tar-filled hands together as if I were hearing some dreadful news.

"Helga, will you be my wife?"

"No!" The words escaped me so abruptly, so brutally.

"Hakon can't marry you."

I said nothing, for at that moment, I understood that I had always thought of myself — even when we were children — as Hakon's wife, not his sister.

"He can't marry a woman whose mother was a

slave." Then he whispered, "I am sorry, Helga."

I could hear that it was true that he felt sorry for me; and this made me angry. "And you, Magnus, can you marry a slave?"

"Yes, I can. My grandmother was a Finn Woman, dark like the forests in the east. They say she kept company with trolls, and that she could read the future."

Magnus was looking down at the sand. I had heard that story before; but I had never believed it, for Magnus' hair was almost white and his skin very fair. "Then because your grandmother was a witch, and my mother a slave, you think we should marry, so that our children can have both a Finn Woman and a slave to brag about as their ancestors?"

"No! No! That is not the reason."

Magnus was looking out over the sea, and his features looked so sad that I said, "I am sorry." Although I did not know what I was sorry about.

"If you marry Hakon, you will always be a slave. If you marry me, you will be free. Each time that Hakon is angry at you, he will remember that once you were a slave."

"That's not true!"

Magnus looked long at me; then shaking his head, he replied, "You are right: Hakon might not think of it. But you will. You will say to yourself, 'Hakon could have married an earl's daughter.' And these words will feel as cold as the winter winds that come from the Land of the Giants."

I felt already that the sweet spring breeze that blew against my cheek had winter's kisses hidden in it, and

56

tears formed in my eyes. "Then I shall marry no one!"

Seeing my tears, Magnus said, "I am sorry. I didn't mean to hurt you."

With the back of my hand, I dried my eyes and left great streaks of tar across my face. "But you did," I whispered; and realizing that my words hurt him, I shouted them, while with my foot I kicked sand at him. "But you did!"

Magnus started to get up; but I did not want to hear any more words. I ran towards the hall, and then passed it, into the birch copse of Odin's. There alone among the trees, I cried my anger and sorrow away.

8

"Wings of the wind,
Odin and Thor,
Smooth the blue road
For our keel.
Let our voyage
Bring glory to Rogen
And shame on no one.
Odin!
Gray one,
Father of men,
Spurn not our gift,
Nor take from us
Our strength."

FROM WHERE I WAS HIDING, behind some bushes, I could not see Hakon, only hear his voice. It was the day of the departure. The morning was beautiful. The wind blew steadily from the mainland, and the sun shone clear in a cloudless sky. It was early, and as I moved my head to try to get a better view, the dew from the branches fell on my face.

All the people of Rogen were collected in Odin's

clearing. They stood in a circle around the big stone, on which was lying a sheep, with its legs tied together. The old people had grumbled when they had heard that only a sheep would be offered. They said that the powers of the gods had grown feeble when a man who owned cows and horses dared set sail on so dangerous a journey and only offer Odin an old sheep. It was not true that the sheep was old; and I believe most of the grumbling came from their stomachs, for they had eaten very little cow meat that winter.

A great cry rose from the people, and drowned out the bleating of the poor sheep. "To Odin!" And a moment later, "To Thor!" I climbed out of my hiding place. A twig caught in my hair. I stopped to take it out; then I ran to the beach. In the still water, near the shore, the longship was lying at anchor. The sail was furled, but ready to be hoisted.

Quickly I took off my clothes. Making a bundle of them I waded into the sea. It was still bitterly cold and felt like needles against my skin. Shivering, I stood still; the water came up to my knees. My plan depended on no one seeing me, so grinding my teeth I walked on until the cold water reached my waist. Then I held the bundle of clothes above my head and ducked my body. Once I was thoroughly wet, I did not feel so cold. I waded to the side of the ship, which was turned away from land; only my head was above the water now. The ship lay high in the water, for it was not heavily loaded. I tried to throw my clothes into it, but the bundle bounced off the railing and fell into the water.

Once more I threw it and this time I heard the bundle fall on the deck of the ship. Now, with both hands free, I could swim.

I tried to reach an oar hole, but my arms were too short. Swimming aft, towards the steering oar, I began to be frightened of getting a cramp. The steering oar was pulled out of the water, and hung just a hand's breadth above it. A little above the blade, I grabbed it, and pulled half my body out of the water. The sun felt warm on my back. I fought desperately not to slide back into the cold sea. Throwing one leg over the oar and using both hands and legs to climb with, I managed to reach the railing. My strength was almost gone when at last I pushed myself over it and into the boat.

I sat down where I had fallen on the deck; breathing very deeply, I began to rub my numb feet. The boat looked very different now. The deck was in place. The oars lay in two long rows, midship. Near the mast lay my bundle of clothes. Bending low so that no one could see me from the shore, I made my way to it. It had not been long enough in the water to be wet thoroughly. I spread the clothes out on the deck, hoping they would dry before I had to hide.

The railing at midship is so low that I could have easily been seen from the shore had not the sail and the heavy spar hidden me from view. I lifted one of the loose deck boards near the mast. Below it were stored all the shields of the men; and though there was room for me, I thought it not a very comfortable place to hide. Replacing this board, I lifted one closer to the bow of the ship. The space was half filled with skins. "A fine bed," I thought. I lifted the board next to the one I had already removed. Now there was room enough for me to squeeze myself in. I sat down upon the skins; only my head was above the deck. I tried to see whether I could put back the planks from below. When the second plank fell into place above me, my hiding place grew dark and I heard for the first time the groaning noises of a ship.

I lay still in the darkness. As my eyes grew accustomed to it, I could see the heavy mast, and the shields and the weapons stored near my feet. Forgetting how low my new home was, I sat up. My head struck against the deck plank. "Wood to wood," I said, but the joke did not please me. I lifted the deck boards aside and climbed out into the world again, but I did not put them back in place perfectly: I let one rest partly on top of the other, so that it would be easier to take them up when I had to hide once more.

I was now completely dry. I turned my woolen dress over: one of the sleeves was still damp. I crawled on all fours under the sail, to the other side of the ship. Through one of the oar holes, I looked at the shore. The beach was still deserted. From the grove of trees where the offering had been made, I saw smoke rise: the women were roasting the sheep. After the offering — the *blot* to Odin — it was customary for all to eat one last meal together. Toasts would be drunk to the success of the voyage; but the mead would be weak, for a drunken crew sets a poor course.

I made my way back to the sheltered side of the ship and sat down, resting my back against the mast. Bending my knees, I hugged them with my arms and leaned my head upon them. I was thinking about Hakon. He was angry with me, for I had refused to take part in the offering. I had told him that I would go to the Mountain of the Sun the day he sailed, and offer my prayers to Odin there. Hakon had raged at me. He had told me that I was stubborn and that he would bring me back nothing from the south. I had replied that the south could offer me nothing that I did not already have. Then he had accused me of not wanting him to win fame, but die a tender of sheep. When he had said that I had become frightened. Gazing into his eyes, I had muttered, "Let me sail with you. When the journey is finished, then tell me that I am a coward!"

Hakon had frowned and shaken his head. "From the Mountain of the Sun, I shall watch the boat sail. There I shall be so far away that you cannot see my tears," I had said.

Hakon had put his hands on my shoulders. "One can bend but never break a willow branch."

I had quickly seen that his mood had changed and smilingly had whispered to him, "Bring me a golden headband from the south."

"Those who do not obey their chieftain shall receive no gift from his hand."

Now — sitting on board the ship — remembering his words made me laugh. "Oh, chieftain, if you only knew how I have disobeyed you!" I giggled and stretched out my legs.

At last my clothes were dry and I put them on. I had brought with me a little leather bag, containing half a loaf of bread and some smoked sheep's meat. I now dropped the bag on top of the skins in my hiding place at the bottom of the boat.

To the mast were tied two oak barrels. On top of each was an opening covered by a square lid. The barrels were filled with water. I took the dipper that hung at the side of one of the barrels, removed the lid, and drank. The water tasted a little of tar; still I drank as much as I could.

I lifted a deck plank, where I thought the pots would be. A smell rose strongly into my nostrils; it was the storage place for the onions. I bent over and took three large onions. Sticking my head through the opening, I could see the pots. They were beneath a plank farther aft. When I removed it, I saw what I wanted: a large wooden drinking cup. I took the cup, put the planks back into their places, gathered up my onions, and walked — bending far forward to prevent myself from being seen — to the water barrels. I filled up the drinking cup almost to the brim and carried it to my hiding place. Wedging it between two piles of skins, I hoped that not all the water would spill once the boat started to sail.

Once again I peeped through an oar hole, to look at the shore. I saw no one. The sun was now quite warm. It was the middle of the morning. Stretching out on the deck I enjoyed the warmth of the sun on my face. In my ears, I could hear the gulls from Grass Island. My eyes watched the top of the mast; it swayed gently, drawing a line on the sky. I thought of Hakon and how angry he would be when he discovered me. Suddenly, Hakon's features changed; and it was Magnus the Fair I saw with my closed eyes. I had fallen asleep.

9

DREAMS DO NOT CARE about the movement of the sun.
In them the past is as real as the present. To some people, life is all dreams — all past — and on these, time has
closed its door. Such a person was Freya the Old. It
was she who had prophesied to me that our ship would
never come home. When I was a child, she had been the
cause of many of my nightmares. Now — that morning
as I lay sleeping on the deck — Freya came to me in
my dreams. She was young and did not resemble the
Freya I knew: the dirty, old woman with matted hair
and deep-set eyes. Yet it was she; I knew this as you do
in dreams. Freya did not talk to me, but looked at me as
if she wanted to warn me: to tell me something that
could not be told. Far away in the dream, a dog barked.
Freya turned her head, as if to listen to the dog; then
she disappeared and I awoke.

The dog was still barking. It was Trold, Hakon's
dog. I leapt to my feet; and then ducked, remembering
that I must not be seen. I could hear the voices of many
men from the beach. I sprang into my hiding place; the
boards were more troublesome to replace this time, for
I was nervous. At the moment when the second board
fell into place, I felt something bump against the side of

the ship. It was one of the smaller boats, bringing the first of the men aboard. I held my breath: I heard the voices of Hakon and Rark. From the shore, I could still hear Trold barking. I thanked my luck that Hakon had decided not to take his dog on board, for surely Trold would have smelled me out and ruined my plan.

"The wind is against us, we shall have to row." It was Hakon, he was standing directly above me. I pressed myself down among the skins, and put one of my hands across my mouth to stifle the cough I was sure would come. My heart was beating so terribly loud that it seemed to fill my hiding place.

"We can row east for a while; then raise the sail and set the course south. The men's hands are not used to the oars. Too much early rowing would give them blisters and discourage the younger men needlessly." At first I could not recognize the voice; but soon I realized that it must be Erp the Traveler, for he was the steersman.

It was not long before all the men were on board. As they trampled about, getting everything ready, the noise beneath the deck frightened me.

Normally, one would sail with a double crew: about sixty men on a ship of *Munin*'s size; but on Rogen, there were not that many men to spare. Hakon's crew was made up of thirty men and four women. The women were young and strong; but several of the men had reached their prime many summers ago, and the snows of winter showed in their beards and hair.

Suddenly everything was still. I realized that the men

had taken their seats, and the oars hovered above the water, waiting for Hakon's command.

"May Odin give us fair winds, and Thor victory!" Hakon's voice came from the aft of the ship. I knew without seeing him that he was standing beside the steersman. His words made a shiver run through my body; and strangely enough, though I felt neither sorrow nor happiness, a tear filled my eye.

"Do not tire yourselves needlessly, by pulling harder on your oar than your neighbor. If you do this, you will only make both his and your own work harder."

Above me, a young man sniggered at Erp the Traveler's warning.

"Anyone who feels like laughing may save his laughter, till the waves turn white with anger and grow as fast as hunger. It will serve him well then, and bring him honor, instead of shaming him."

Everyone respected Erp, and knew that in him *Munin* had a better steersman than most ships that would sail the sea that summer; so they were all silent, even the young man above me.

"We will sail, with course towards the mainland, until the sun shines from the west; then we will raise the sail and our course will be south, until the sun rises."

A few moments later, after what seemed like a long silence, came Hakon's command: "Let down the steering oar!" Again there was silence. "Pull up the anchor!"

The ship glided forward as the men pulled on the anchor's rope. I heard the anchor bump against the side of the ship and the men cry, "Anchor up!"

"Oars ready . . . Row!" As Hakon shouted the last word of the command, the oars struck the water and the ship started moving forward. From shore came the shouts of the people, wishing the Vikings luck. Hakon's Trold was barking and whining. I could imagine him running along the beach, for Trold would not swim in the water when it was winter-cold.

I arranged myself as comfortably as I could, with my hands folded behind my head. "The voyage has begun," I said to myself; and though I smiled, I was also trembling.

The noises of the moving ship filled my ears. The boards of the hull groaned as the waves knocked with their fingers on its sides; and the oars squeaked in the oar holes as the men pulled them.

"Tomorrow, I shall come out; then we shall be far south," I thought.

Remembering that I had not eaten since that morning, I took a little bread and ate an onion. I thought of Harold the Bowbender and how angry he would be when he could not find me. I did not doubt that he would guess where I was; nor would he really think less of me for it. His only sons, Nils and Eigil, were on board the ship. Harold would be lonely, but he would never show it. At that moment, I was glad I was a girl — even a slave girl — for I was free to weep or not, as I chose. "Surely, he did not want them to go." I whispered the words, for it made me feel less lonely to talk. I remembered the saying: "The sparrow has a song;

only the eagle is silent." Again, I spoke aloud: "Then it is better to be a sparrow."

I heard footsteps above me: two people were walking midship. When they came to the mast, they paused. "Helga will be disappointed." It was Hakon's voice. "She thought we would sail past the Mountain of the Sun."

"And you, Hakon, won't you be disappointed — you expected to see her?"

I held my breath while I waited for Hakon to answer Rark's question.

"I would have taken her with me, Rark . . ."

As I said under my breath, "Why didn't you?" Rark echoed my words above me.

"What have my father and I ever brought her but harm?"

I wanted to shout through the planks, "You have never done me any harm!"

"I could not risk her life," Hakon continued. "She is my little sister. The gods do not have the power they used to. She will be safer with Harold the Bowbender on Rogen . . . Besides, I like the thought that she is at home."

Rark laughed. "Waiting for you?" he said jokingly.

Now Hakon also laughed. As they turned and started walking towards the stern, Hakon remarked, "Poor is the man, though Earl be his title, who has no person waiting for him."

Hakon's words made me happy, but also ashamed. If by wishing I could have returned to Rogen, I would have. But no bird has ever flown with wishes as its wings.

I waited for Hakon and Rark to return midship; but they did not. Soon the monotonous noise of the waves against the hull made my eyes close in spite of my will, and I fell asleep.

10

I woke when the men stopped rowing and the sail was hoisted. The course had been altered. Some of the pots and pans that had not been stored carefully enough slid, with a great clatter, the width of the ship as *Munin*, being under sail, heeled to starboard. The waves, which the ship before had stamped against, now splashed her side.

A group of the crew seated themselves above my hiding place. I listened to their talk. It was gay and filled with good-natured jokes about each other. They compared the sizes of their blisters on their hands, and the younger ones boasted of the Viking deeds they would do in the south.

"I thought that I had set sail with men. I must have been mistaken. This old boat must be Valhalla, populated with heroes and gods." (Even if I had not recognized his voice, I would have known from what was said that it was Magnus the Fair who was speaking.) "Tell me, Thorkild, you know the story of Volund the Blacksmith, who killed the sons of his enemy, King Nidud. Do you think him brave?"

Thorkild had been the loudest at bragging; but he

was better known for his good nature than his courage. He laughed and said, " 'Volund the Blacksmith' is a tale told on winter nights. Who knows whether he — or King Nidud — ever lived."

Magnus laughed, too. "And we are we; but what shall we be when our bones are moldering, and our only life is in our grandchildren's tongues?" He paused and then declaimed one of the verses from the Saga of Volund the Blacksmith.

> "With cunning and wile,
> The blacksmith enticed
> To his isle,
> King Nidud's children.
> For father's crimes,
> The young were slain.
> Volund laughed,
> Made from their skulls
> Drinking cups,
> To toast the Gods."

No one spoke; then Magnus, himself, argued: "King Nidud had done Volund much harm. He had stolen his gold, and made a cripple of him by cutting the muscles in both his legs. But King Nidud's sons were children, who had done Volund no evil. To drink mead from an enemy's skull may be pleasing to those whose anger is as limitless as the sea; but what god should care to have his toast drunk from the skulls of children?"

Again everyone was silent; then I heard Orm the Storyteller say, "A song is merely a song: a tale, a tale. If each word had to be weighed on your scales, Magnus, then all men would be mute."

One of the men stood up. I guessed that it was Magnus. "It is ill when the tongue sings of deeds that the hand should not stoop to." I heard Magnus walk towards the stern of the ship.

As soon as he was out of earshot, the men started to laugh and talk again. I said to myself, "They are like children, when the grownup has left." I thought of Magnus and the Finn Woman, who was his grandmother; and I felt cold, for it is said that the Finn Woman knew the future and could speak with the wind.

Soon the men above me stopped talking and stretched out upon the deck. Wrapped in their cloaks, they must have fallen asleep. I drank some water, nibbled at some bread, and closed my eyes. But Magnus' words kept me from sleeping; for a long time, I lay there thinking of tales and sagas.

I woke many times during the night. I was cold and unused to being on board a ship. By morning, I was not feeling well. The skins that had been my bed had only been rudely tanned and had an unpleasant smell. The sail must have been taken down; I could hear the oars once more, and I supposed that the course had been changed.

It had been my plan to wait until midday to climb from my shelter; but when a particularly heavy wave made the ship pitch even more wildly than before, I threw aside the two boards above me and stood up.

The first thing I saw was the surprised face of Ketil

Ragnvaldson, who was sitting on his wooden chest and rowing, near the hole out of which I had so suddenly appeared. So surprised was Ketil that he forgot his oar and it slipped out of the water. Since he had been pulling on it with all his strength, he lost his balance and fell backward. Some of the men started to laugh and several stopped rowing. Erp the Traveler's stern voice brought them back to work.

"Row . . . Row . . . Row . . ." he shouted, and soon all the men were rowing evenly again.

I looked around for Hakon. I was standing, facing aft, and I had not seen him, though he was sitting only a few feet behind me talking to Rark and Magnus. He and the others around him looked at me with such astonishment as they would have at a troll.

"I'm sorry," I mumbled. As nobody replied, I repeated my apology a little louder: "I'm sorry."

I believe it was Hakon's amazement that made him say, "Where have you come from?"

The question made Magnus the Fair laugh. "From Valhalla, Hakon Olafson. She is one of Odin's Valkyries, who has come to bring you victory in battle."

Hakon held up his hand, as a sign that he did not want anyone but himself to speak. "Why did you disobey me?"

Now I was feeling very sick, indeed. The onion and the bread I had eaten yesterday seemed no longer willing to stay in my stomach. I held one hand in front of my mouth, and with the help of the other scrambled across the deck to the side of the ship. "It was a bad onion," I mumbled as I threw up all of yesterday's meals. Hanging over the railing, I saw the sea's green back so near that I could touch it.

Two hands grabbed me, dragged me over to the mast, and laid me down upon some skins. "Close your eyes, it sometimes helps."

I opened my eyes wide and stared into Hakon's kind face. He covered me with a cloak and smiled down at me. "I am sorry," I said again. As I closed my eyes, I thought how lucky it was that I had become seasick, for no one could be angry at me now.

When I next awoke, it was nearly noon. The wind had jumped and *Munin* was moving under sail again. The shifting of the wind had calmed the sea. I felt much better; even a little hungry. The men were lying about the deck in small groups. I noticed that several of them were pale. Near me, I saw Rark. His face was white; he was lying on his back and his eyes were closed. It gave me comfort to know that I was not the only one who was sick, for seasickness is not like other illnesses. It makes you feel ridiculous and ashamed, as if it were a personal weakness, for which you can find no excuse.

I sat up. Magnus the Fair was standing at the steering oar. Near him Hakon and Erp the Traveler were sitting. I got up, but I would have fallen down immediately if I had not had to steady me one of the ropes that pulled up the sail. I looked at the tilted deck and dared not let go of the rope. Hakon noticed me. With a wave of his hand, he told me to wait, while he himself got up and walked forward to me. With pride, I saw how easily he walked and that his cheeks were rosy.

Hakon did not scold me, as I expected him to. He seemed to have forgotten how I had joined the crew of *Munin*. He asked me if I felt better, and I nodded.

"Tomorrow evening we shall see land, and the day after we shall be in Tronhjem." He turned his head upward towards the sail. "That is, if the wind keeps." He seemed so serious. "In Tronhjem, we shall see Thora." As he looked out over the sea, I remembered how much he had loved his stepmother. "And I hope, Gunhild, your mother."

"Yes," I whispered, for I dared say no more, because I had not given my mother a thought.

Hakon misunderstood my silence. His heart was purer than mine. He could not imagine that my mother's lack of affection for me had long since killed my love for her. "I hope we shall find her well," he said consolingly. "I shall buy her free."

"Yes," I mumbled. "Thank you." I felt bitterly ashamed, for my first thought had been, "I don't want her on board this ship; she will make me a slave again!" For I thought that my mother Gunhild could never be free. Her heart, her spirit, would be forever the slave's; and I did not believe that it would even please her to see her daughter escape from that bondage that had broken herself.

But Hakon lived in a world of day and night: twilight did not exist. The world was a battleground between good and evil.

"Before we left, I offered a hare to Balder." Balder was Hakon's favorite god. It was he who would reign, when all the other gods were gone and man lived in peace with his fellow men.

"You did well," I said and smiled, as though I were a mother whose child had done a good deed.

"I told no one," Hakon explained. "I was afraid that they might laugh at me. Now the thought has come to me that I was wrong, that I might have offended Balder by being ashamed of my offering." Hakon's brow was knitted.

I grabbed one of his hands in both of mine, and said, "I am sorry I disobeyed you."

Hakon smiled and his face cleared. "Little sister, I am glad you are here. We have never been apart. I would have missed you."

I bent my head.

"Hakon Olafson!" With relief, I heard Erp the Traveler's voice, and let go of Hakon's hand.

Hakon rose, but before he walked aft, his hand rested for a moment on mine. Again I marveled at the ease with which he crossed the deck of the moving ship. Without holding on to the railing, he now stood talking with Erp. It was time to change steersman, and it was obviously Hakon's turn to stand at the oar. As Hakon grabbed the steering pin that protruded from the top of the heavy steering oar, the man who had stood at the oar stretched himself and looked at the sky. It was Magnus the Fair and he appeared as indifferent to the movement of *Munin* as Hakon. Somehow, it did not make me happy; I wished that Magnus were as sick as Rark.

11

THE WIND blew steadily from the sea toward the land, and we arrived at the opening of the fjord that leads to Tronhjem four days after we had left Rogen. On an island in the mouth of the fjord, we camped for the night. The men were glad to stretch their legs again, and the younger ones started to run races on the beach. The island was deserted by man, but not by the birds of the sea. Screaming, they flew about protesting against our invasion. Many ships must have landed on this island before us, for we found several rings of fire-blackened stones.

As it had not rained for many days, the driftwood was dry; and soon, we had a fire burning. Hakon had not taken many supplies with him from Rogen, for he intended to buy them in Tronhjem, but he had brought two freshly slaughtered yearling lambs. These were now roasted. During the last few days, we had eaten nothing but smoked meat, onions, and stale bread, and we could hardly wait for the lambs to be thoroughly cooked.

I gathered wood and then tended the fire with the other women. Besides myself, there were four: Gretha, the wife of Hakon the Black, a strong but silent woman, with a kind heart; she was only a few years older than myself. Freya the Young, thirty summers old, to whom no man had yet dared speak of marriage; she was as strong as a man and had a sharp tongue. Astrid Erpsdaughter, who was the oldest daughter of Erp the Traveler; she and I, from early childhood, had been friends. The fourth was Rigmor Ragnvaldsdaughter; her brother Ketil was also among the crew. Her father, Ragnvald Harelip, had been loyal to the tyrant, Sigurd Sigurdson, when he ruled Rogen; and it was Ragnvald who had killed Sven the Dane, while we all stood waiting for Hakon to pass judgment on him. Although Rigmor was my own age, I hardly knew her.

While we were busy preparing the food, I noticed that Rigmore preferred not to work at my side; and once, when I smiled to her, she turned her face away. "It is good to know your friends, but second best, to know your enemies," I thought. And I made no more attempts to be friendly with Rigmor Ragnvaldsdaughter.

Early the next morning, we left the island and set sail for Tronhjem. As the fjord became narrower, the wind died and we had to row. I was sitting in the bow with Astrid Erpsdaughter and Gretha, Hakon the Black's wife. Filled with excitement, we were looking towards the shore. We saw several small boats, whose crews were fishing; and on land, we saw many buildings.

Munin was now only being rowed by sixteen oars, so many of the crew were free to look and marvel at what there was to be seen. The older men were pointing out to the younger ones, most of whom had never been outside Rogen, what hall belonged to which family.

Magnus the Fair and Ketil Ragnvaldson came up to us. "Soon, Ketil, we shall see women fairer than we are used to. They say that Earl Hakon has more wives than we have women on Rogen." Magnus was talking to Ketil as if we were not there at all.

Astrid answered him by remarking to Gretha, "They say the boys in Earl Hakon's hird are so strong that in the rest of Norway they would count for men. It is also said that the men are so big that they must walk, for no horse can carry them."

Magnus was silent for a moment and very thoughtful; then he turned to Ketil: "The women of Tronhjem spin gold. They can weave more in a day than our women can in a year."

Ketil, who until now had said nothing, joined the game. "They say they are so wonderfully strong, too, that the Valkyries who dwell with Odin all come from Tronhjem."

From behind Magnus and Ketil came the voice of Freya the Young. Laughing, she said loudly, "We must take care of our men, Helga; lest these women should think them babes and put them to sleep among their infants."

Ketil's face grew red, but Magnus only grinned. "If the women of Tronhjem are so strong, I shall stay close to Freya the Young, and she shall protect me."

A ship as big as *Munin* was sighted. It had a dragon's head mounted in its bow. The ship passed so near us that we could see the faces of the men. Erp knew the name of the chieftain. It was Orm Lyrgia, who was wellborn and rich. Erp hailed him. He did not answer, but sailed on. His course was toward Bunes, where he had his hall.

Late in the afternoon we cast anchor, a little southeast of Tronhjem. Hakon decided that he would wait the night on board *Munin*. In the morning he would visit Earl Hakon. Sigrid, Hakon's mother, had been a cousin of the mighty Earl; Hakon built much hope on this kinship. We knew that the Earl was in Tronhjem, for we had seen his ship, at anchor among five other longships.

Now that *Munin* was at anchor, the shields were put up alongside the railing. The first shield on the starboard side was Hakon's. From the mast flew Hakon's banner, a blue cloth with Odin's raven, Munin, in black. Out of the sail a tent was made, midship. The little boat that had lain on the foremost part of the deck was put in the water and fastened aft.

The men were all eager to go ashore, and Hakon's orders had disappointed them; but he gave out a double measure of mead, and soon only the guards on *Munin* were awake.

When the sun rose over the mountains in the east, not a cloud disrupted the blueness of the sky. The winds were asleep, or gone to some other place to whip the waves. *Munin* mirrored itself perfectly in the water, which was so still that one could clearly see, far below her hull, the boulders and the seaweed at the bottom of the sea. As soon as the sun had fully risen, all were awake. After a hasty meal of bread and smoked fish, we started to prepare ourselves for going ashore.

It was soon obvious that if every man had his will, the ship would be left unguarded; therefore Hakon divided the crew into three groups. One was to go ashore with him; another was to stay on board the ship; and the third was to make a camp on the beach and prepare the midday meal. To command the men on board the ship, Hakon appointed Hakon the Black; to lead those who were to make the camp, Ketil Ragnvaldson. Among the group which was to follow Hakon to Earl Hakon's hall, besides the older men, were: Magnus the Fair, Rark, and the two sons of Harold the Bowbender. Since Hakon had not called my name, I did not know to which group I belonged. I had not even dared to hope that he would take me with him to the great Earl's hall.

I was amazed when Hakon said, "You'll come with me, Helga."

"Yes," I whispered. Then behind me I heard a woman's voice whisper, "A chieftain needs a slave to attend him." But I had not the courage to turn around.

Those who were to go with Hakon made much out of their dressing. Magnus the Fair insisted that Astrid Erpsdaughter should cut his hair and beard. The men found this a sight to their taste, and crowded around Magnus and Astrid, giving advice as to the hair style that would best suit him.

"The shape of a hen's egg is most pleasing," said Astrid. She grabbed as much of Magnus' hair as she could hold in one hand, while with the other she brought the scissors near his head. Magnus sat perfectly still — dar-

ing her to do it, by appearing unconcerned. Astrid let
his hair fall, and admitted her defeat by starting to cut
it very carefully and skillfully. Later she told me that if
Magnus had said one word, or had tried to protect his
locks with his hands, she would have cut them off.

I had only the one wool dress I had carried with me
when I sneaked on board *Munin*. I washed myself
much and combed my hair, which fell to my shoulders
but was not yet long enough to be braided. Gretha,
who was to stay behind with her husband, Hakon the
Black, noticed the plainness of my dress and loaned me
a silver brooch. I was very grateful to Gretha. I fastened the brooch to my dress below my neck. I had
never had a brooch before; I was nervous; and I put it
on crooked.

Gretha took it out again and refastened it. When she
had finished, she said softly, "You must not mind Rigmor. She is only jealous."

I looked up at Gretha. So it was Rigmor who had
whispered that a chieftain must have a slave to attend
him. "Why should she be jealous of me?" I asked; for
truly my heart was still too much of a child's to know
of a woman's passion.

"She loves Magnus the Fair. Didn't you know?" My
expression must have been answer enough for Gretha.
She laughed kindly and kissed me on the cheek.

"Bring the boat alongside," Hakon called. One of
the men drew the small boat up midship of *Munin*.
Two of the shields were removed from the railing.
Hakon and the older men climbed over the side and
into the boat.

There was not room for all of us in the small boat, and it had to return a second time. I was the last to step up to the railing. When I hesitated before jumping, Magnus the Fair held up his hands.

My foot slipped and I fell into the arms of Magnus. He and the other men laughed; but I quickly freed myself and made my way to the stern. My face was red and I felt ashamed, though I did not know why. As the boat pulled away from *Munin*, I looked back at the ship. Rigmor Ragnvaldsdaughter was standing in the bow of *Munin*, following us with her eyes. I looked down at my hands. Knotting them and unknotting them, I whispered, "I am sorry."

12

As we walked to Earl Hakon's hall, many people
came out of their dwellings to see us. According to the
standards of Rogen we were richly dressed. But someone said as we passed, "They look like a group of
farmers, from mountains where the grazing is so poor
that a man counts himself rich if he owns a cow." The
awareness of our poverty made us walk close together,
and look at the people about us as if they were our enemies. Though Hakon was almost as tall as a full-grown
man, his father's great sword, that he wore from his
belt, made him seem small. Only Erp the Traveler
seemed undisturbed; but he was known in Tronhjem,
and had some fame as a steersman, even here.

I had been told so much about the hall of Earl
Hakon that when I finally saw it, I was disappointed.
True, it was at least five times the size of our hall on
Rogen. Still the materials that had been used in its making were the same, while the hall I had built in my imag-
ination had not been limited by beams or boards or
stones. The doors of the entrance impressed us all; and
it was not alone because of their size — though they
were twice as tall as a man, and when they were open,
four men could enter abreast — but they were beauti-

fully carved and there was a ring of gold that opened the latch. Of this ring, many men had spoken. Its weight in gold was such that it could have purchased three longships the size of *Munin*.

One of the older men, Sigmund the Hairless, who had — already as a very young man — lost all the hair on his head, let his fingers glide around it, caressing it gently as a woman does her firstborn. "That ring has caused many a man to have evil dreams," he said, and returned his hand to the hilt of his sword, as if he had burned it.

"Gold, though soft and of little use, is yet stronger than the steel of a sword." We had all turned to look at the speaker of these words. He stood a few steps from us, and gazed at us with such contempt that he seemed proud of not hiding it. He was not tall, but was very broadly built. He must have been strong when young, but the eating of too much pork had made him fat. He wore no sword or weapon of any kind. His dress was a mixture of very costly materials and very plain wool.

Erp the Traveler whispered something to Hakon. Hakon glanced unbelievingly at the stranger and said, "Go tell your master that Hakon Olafson of Rogen is here and wants to speak with him."

The man did not move; but smiled back insolently, as if he had not heard what Hakon had said.

"Earl Hakon must have a kind heart, to keep such a slave about him."

Hakon's remark made me look at the man with wonder: Was he a slave? The green cloak that was flung over his shoulders was finer than the blue one that

Hakon wore. "It is Kark," Magnus whispered in my ear; and then to make certain I understood what he meant, he added, "Earl Hakon's slave."

All of us had heard of Kark, who had been born on the same night as the Earl, and had always been his slave. Kark was tied to his master, as a shadow is to a man; but like the shadow, Kark mirrored that part of the Earl's soul that grown men shuddered to think about. It was said that it was Kark who on the order of his master had killed Earl Hakon's own son, Erling, to offer him to the Valkyrie (whose name is Torgerde Holgasbride) in order to win victory over the Vikings of Jomscastle. But the ear should not trust all that it hears, for other people have said that Erling was Earl Hakon's favorite son and that he had died of a cough. The story of the offering of Erling, these people claim, was invented by the Earl's enemies, who believe in the new god.

"My memory is not what it used to be," Kark was saying. "What was your name? It passed by me like a summer breeze."

Hakon's face grew red with anger, but he kept his temper. "Hakon Olafson of Rogen is my name. Go and tell your master I want to speak with him . . . But hurry, lest the summer breeze turn into a winter wind."

By now a lot of people had gathered around us, and Kark knew that it would not displease them if he made fools of the ill-clad strangers from the north. "Make way for the mighty Chief of Rogen, Earl of Sheep and Cod, ruler of the Kingdom of the Gulls."

The people laughed boisterously. Hakon drew his

sword. Kark looked for a moment at the drawn weapon. Then — perhaps because I was standing so near Hakon — he kneeled down in front of me. "Queen of the Island of Fog and Rain, protect me from your master!" Kark looked up at me. His lips were twisted in a grin. His eyes shifted their gaze often, for he was trying to judge the impression his performance was making.

"He has a head like a troll," I thought.

"Protect your poor slave!" Kark mockingly held up his hands towards me. On one of his fingers he wore a gold ring; but his hands had grown so fat that the ring was all but encased in flesh.

"Poor you are not, but slave you are!" And in anger and repulsion, I struck his face as hard as I could with my hand.

A great shout went up from the people around me, and some of the men called, "Hit him again!"

"Who breaks the peace of the morning?" The door to the hall had been opened, and all of us turned to see the speaker, who stood on the top step. I knew, without being told, that it was Earl Hakon Sigurdson, called Earl Hakon the Rich. He had inherited from his father, Earl Sigurd the Good, the ability to make all men around him seem small and unimportant; yet he was not a tall man, nor was he handsome. He was untidily dressed, obviously he had only just woken up. Neither his beard nor his brown hair, which was streaked with gray, had yet been combed. Around his waist he wore a belt of gold. The plainness of the rest of his garments somehow gave more luster to the gold.

Kark ran to his master, and kneeling in front of him said, "King Olaf Trygveson has come with an army to beg your pardon, mighty Earl, and to offer with you to the gods!"

King Olaf was Earl Hakon's bitterest enemy; and the Earl had sworn to Odin that he would kill him. When Kark realized that his joke had not pleased his master, he began to mumble who we were.

Hakon put his sword back in his belt and stepped forward. "I am Hakon Olafson of Rogen. Ten times has son followed father as ruler of that island. My mother's name was Sigrid, Sigrid Hakonsdaughter. Her father came from Tronhjem and called the mighty Earl Sigurd brother."

We all watched the Earl's face intently. It was furrowed, as if he were trying to find something in his memory that he feared was lost. "Your mother, I remember her," he said at last.

The Earl had spoken quietly; yet there was not one of us from Rogen who had not heard him, and even Erp the Traveler sighed his relief. Earl Hakon seemed to be speaking more to himself than to us, as if he were using words as torches, to lead him through a dark passage. "Her hair was yellow and she was taller than I was. Sigrid . . . Sigrid . . ." He repeated the name, as if it were something eatable. "Be welcome to my hall, Cousin . . . Who is the girl with you?"

Hakon waited a moment before answering, and I drew back and hid behind Magnus the Fair. "She is a woman of my island."

Earl Hakon laughed and said to his young kinsman,

"If our blood is kin, then many a woman will shed tears over you before you go to Odin's Hall." Now he turned to me. "Step forward, girl; and let me see what the women on my cousin's island look like."

I stepped forward, but kept my gaze at my feet.

"A pity you are not a slave." I shuddered, but I made myself look up, fearing that my lack of courage would speak of my birth. "If you were a slave," the Earl continued, "I should buy you, and marry you to Kark, so that his ears might be warmed every day."

Kark was still kneeling at his master's feet. The repulsion I felt for him came back to me and made me bold. "We have an old she-goat on Rogen that is too tough for slaughter; if your slave wishes to marry an equal, we shall take it with us when next we come to Tronhjem."

Earl Hakon laughed and turning to Hakon, said, "The north wind that beats on Rogen sharpens your women's tongues . . . Will you and your hird eat the midday meal with us, Hakon Olafson?"

"We shall deem it an honor, Earl Hakon Sigurdson, and when we grow old we shall say with pride, 'We have once been guests in Earl Hakon's hall.'" Hakon's words pleased the Earl, for like most men, he did not think a flatterer an empty-handed guest. "Till then!"

Earl Hakon smiled and nodded. He beckoned to his slave, Kark, to follow him into the hall; but as he was about to enter, he paused, and then spoke without turning his head: "Bring the girl. Wit in women is so rare that even an Earl does not meet it twice a year."

When the slave, Kark, had closed the door behind his

master, Rark came up to me. "Beware of that man, Helga, and beware of his slave. For though he spits on Kark while all men can see it, in secret the Earl will hold council with him. A man who thinks he grows by kicking slaves has not a free mind or a good heart."

I looked at Rark: had we not both been slaves? Did he think that the beatings I had received had taught me nothing? "I hate the Earl and his slave, too!"

"I know, but you must not show your hatred." Rark shook his head, as I had seen him shake it at Hakon when he was teaching Hakon how to shoot with a bow and arrow, and he missed the target. "It was foolish of you to have hit the slave. Your blow will be ringing in his ears for many days to come, and may cause us much mischief."

Hakon, who was standing near us, listening, came closer to me and put his arm around my shoulder. "Rark worries lest we should all be killed and he not see his father's hall. You did well, little sister."

Hakon's words were unkind. It was true Rark wanted to go home, to his own land in the south; but I do not think he would have hesitated a moment before giving up his life to protect Hakon.

Rark smiled; the kind of smile that comes to a father's face when his son behaves as if he had outgrown him; a smile that is certain to annoy that son.

"Come," Hakon said, "let us go and see if we can't find out how my stepmother, Thora, fares." And he walked over to a group of men, who were standing not far away, and asked them the way to Magnus Thorsen's hall.

13

ONE OF THE younger men among that group whom Hakon had approached offered to show us the way to Magnus Thorsen's hall. He told us that it was called Hjalte Gudbrandson's hall now, for Magnus had died the winter after he had sent Rolf Blackbeard and Ulv Erikson to invade Rogen. His grandson, Hjalte Gudbrandson, now sat in the high seat. Both of Magnus' sons had been lost on a trip to Iceland. When we asked news of Thora, we were told that she was married to Ulv Erikson.

"But she hated him!" The words had burst out of Hakon.

"Some women can be bought with gold," explained the stranger.

"Not Thora!" Hakon replied threateningly.

The young man shrugged his shoulder and turned. He was about to walk away; but as he stepped aside, he must have caught a glimpse of Hakon's face, and realized that Hakon was more unhappy than he was angry. "Come," he said not unkindly, "I said I would take you to Hjalte's hall."

On top of a hill, as we passed what looked to be the ruins of a hall, he stopped. "Magnus Thorsen believed in the new god." He pointed to the stone foundations and the blackened posts that were all that remained of what once had been a building. "That was one of the houses to the new god. Earl Hakon ordered it to be burned and all the priests killed. The Earl made all the men who believed in the new god forswear him and make offerings to Odin. Magnus Thorsen was willing enough, but Earl Hakon also wanted Magnus' gold. Magnus was not quite so willing to forswear his gold as he was his god. Ulv Erikson's star shone very brightly in Earl Hakon's heaven; and Ulv promised to speak to his master for Magnus if he — Ulv — could wed Thora. It was a bargain among three men's greed, that only Thora lost. I believe she did it for her brother's son's sake. Only one of Magnus' sons had married before setting sail for Iceland; and his — Gudbrand's — wife had died in childbirth. All that remained to remind Magnus that he had ever had any sons was Hjalte, then eighteen summers old.

"Magnus died one full moon after Thora's wedding. They say it is because he choked on the bone of a chicken. Well, Tronhjem was the winner and Hades the loser, by his death. There is Hjalte's hall." The young man waved his arm toward a group of buildings occupying the top of a hillock. "I shall not go with you any farther, for I care not for Hjalte; nor he for me. But if it is hunger that drives you to Hjalte's hall, you'd better turn around and find some other friend, for when you leave, you will be hungrier than when you came." With these words and a nod of the head, the young man left us.

Hjalte Gudbrandson's hall was large; but the building was in ill-repair and had a deserted look about it. One of the front doors was open and I noticed, as we entered, that the bottom hinge was broken.

From the twilight darkness of the innermost part of the hall, a voice greeted us: "What do you want? We are poor people. There is nothing to steal here."

"Hakon of Rogen does not steal." Hakon's voice echoed throughout the hall; but no one answered him, and for a moment, I thought that I had imagined the voice and that the hall was empty. "Who are you that calls a stranger thief?" Again only silence answered Hakon.

I looked back towards the open door. The sunlight that shone through it made me wish myself outside again.

"I want to speak with Hjalte Gudbrandson," Hakon called into the stillness. The quiet had made the men afraid, and I noticed that all held their hands upon their swords.

At last came an answer. It was spoken haltingly and high, as a child speaks: "He is gone."

Hakon turned to Rark, but Rark only shook his head.

"Who are you?" It was Magnus the Fair who had spoken; and we all waited for the voice to answer, but it had grown silent again. At the same moment, all of us had the same thought, and we walked towards that dark corner of the hall from whence the voice had come. A pealing, wild laughter stopped us quicker than the sight of twelve armed men would have. All but

Rark drew their swords; even I fingered at the knife that hung from my belt.

The laughter stopped. Again we heard a voice coming from the same place; but this time, it sounded like a man's — high like a woman's, yet like a man's.

"Have you come to avenge your father, Hakon Olafson?"

So unprepared was Hakon for this accusation that he could not speak. I do not think that Hakon had ever thought of avenging his father's death: partly, because he knew that Olaf Sigurdson had given Magnus cause for vengeance by stealing Thora; and partly because Hakon was too young and too poor to attack someone as rich and powerful as Magnus Thorsen.

"Magnus is dead," Rark said.

There was laughter; but it did not sound as mad or as frightening as before. "My father's father has gone to his god. They say his hall is built of gold."

From beneath a pile of skins that was lying in the innermost part of the hall, a huge, white, hairless head stuck out.

"My father's father would like that: the gold. All men like gold, don't they?"

Hjalte Gudbrandson — for it was he! — did not close his mouth when he finished speaking, but left his lips parted, as if it were too much trouble to press them together.

"Some like their honor better," said Magnus the Fair; though he did not seem to be answering Hjalte but merely stating a well-known truth.

Two little arms, like those of a child five summers

old, followed the head out from underneath the skins. "With gold you can buy anything," he repeated, as if the words were part of a curse or one of those rhymes that are taught to children.

When Hjalte Gudbrandson sat up, we all took a step backward. The upper part of his body was bare, and though it was not deformed, it reminded me of the kind of worm that lives in meat when it is rotten. His legs, which he now drew out from underneath the skins, were like his arms: no bigger than a child's.

Looking at our faces, Hjalte laughed. To Hakon, he said, "Well, do you want revenge?" When Hakon, too shocked to answer, remained silent, Hjalte said, with a bit of anger hidden in his voice, "Then put back your sword."

As Hakon returned his sword to his belt, his cheeks grew red. I thought it was anger that had colored his face; but later I realized that it was shame.

"Gudrun!" Hjalte screamed. From a little door in the back of the hall, an elderly woman entered. She came so quickly that she must have been listening, waiting for him to call.

"Get some mead for our guests. They may be thirsty, having traveled so far to see us." With much difficulty, Hjalte walked to the high seat at the end of the table and seated himself. As he passed near me, I drew back; and he smiled, although he did not glance at me.

With some surprise I noticed that the woman was not a dwarf, or a giant, or some other monster, but an old woman of usual proportions, who was richly dressed. On Hjalte's shoulders she now carefully laid a cape of red, glossy material. I had never seen cloth like it before. "You think it pretty, girl?" Hjalte asked.

I nodded, for I was trembling too much to speak.

"It comes from a country at the edge of the world, and I know no man in Tronhjem who has any like it." This thought must have pleased Hjalte enormously, for he grinned and repeated it; "No, no man in Tronhjem has one like it." He waited; when no one else spoke, he added, as an afterthought, "When I die, I shall be buried in it."

Gudrun (who we later were told was his grandmother: that is, his mother's mother, for his father's mother had died long ago) brought us each a cup of mead.

From one to another of us, Hjalte's glance passed, ending with Hakon, who was standing at his side. "To your luck, Hakon Olafson!"

The mead was watery and bitter; in its making, the honey had been used sparingly.

"Drink, Hakon, drink! Or is it not sweet enough?" Hjalte asked.

"You do not overwork your bees, Hjalte Gudbrandson," said Magnus the Fair, and spat some of the drink out on the ground.

Hakon glanced at Magnus disapprovingly.

"It does not matter, there's more mead," Hjalte said, as if Hakon's angry frown had been words that one had to answer.

"I came to ask news of your father's sister, Thora Magnusdaughter."

"She is married to Ulv Erikson." Slowly, he leaned forward towards Hakon. "Yes, she is married to Ulv Hunger. It is a marriage between a dog and a cat . . . Ulv Erikson is my friend, don't you think so?"

Hakon was taken aback by the unexpected question, and Rark answered for him: "Does Ulv have any friends?"

This reply, which was a question, made Hjalte laugh. "Oh, yes. He is my friend; though I am not his friend." Hjalte laughed satisfiedly, as a little child does when he has told a riddle to which he is sure the grownups will not guess the solution.

"When Magnus died, I buried his gold." Saying this made Hjalte laugh so hard that he almost choked. "I never told anyone where I buried it. Now Ulv does not dare kill me, or he will lose Magnus' gold. So he is my friend, for he is a friend to Magnus' gold."

"You could not have buried it deeply or far from here," said Magnus the Fair.

"My grandmother and Sven, the slave, helped me. When Sven had dug the hole and put the gold down into it, my grandmother killed him as he was climbing out . . . Sven liked gold, and now he is as rich as my father's father, Magnus Thorsen." Hjalte looked around at us; he was pleased to see the horror on our faces.

"A pity your grandmother didn't kill you," Erp the Traveler said. Erp rose from his place on the bench, emptied his cup of mead on the ground, and walked out of the hall.

"If you want money for your father's death, go and ask Ulv Erikson for it." Hjalte looked slyly up at Hakon. "He has one hundred men in his hird, all stronger than yours."

When we saw Hakon rise, we all jumped up from our places.

"I can think of no worse revenge than letting you live, Hjalte Gudbrandson!"

As we walked from the hall, we could hear Hjalte laugh, as if Hakon's parting words had been a joke that pleased him very much.

14

THE SUNLIGHT almost blinded us when we came outside; and we stood still for a long moment, while our
eyes became accustomed to it. From one of the huts,
close to the main hall, a slave was staring at us with the
eyes of a dog who fears strangers.

"Sven!"

We all became like stone when we heard that name;
and it was a while before any of us turned to see who
the caller had been.

In the door of the hall stood Gudrun, Hjalte's grandmother. She looked past us, as if we did not exist. The
slave came slowly towards her: was it age or fear that
made him walk so haltingly? The old woman turned
and walked inside again. The slave she had called Sven
followed her without looking back.

"Not everything can be bought with gold," said
Eigil, the oldest son of Harold the Bowbender.

"Were you not frightened?" Hakon asked me.

I glanced over my shoulder at the hall. Now it
looked like any other hall, and held no more terror for
me. "Yes, I was. Do you think it was true that he buried Magnus' gold, and that his grandmother killed the
slave?"

Hakon shrugged his shoulders. "The lust for gold makes men mad. Many a man has done worse deeds for a treasure smaller than the one they say Magnus Thorsen owned."

I thought about Hakon's explanation, but it did not satisfy me: had Hjalte's grandmother called the slave Sven so that we would think her grandson a liar, or just to confuse us? Or was his name merely by chance the same as the slave's whom Hjalte had said his grandmother had killed?

"What does it bring him . . . the gold, I mean?"

Rark, who was walking on one side of me, answered, "What does the silver brooch Gretha loaned you give you?"

Rark's argument annoyed me. "The two things have nothing to do with each other," I said hastily.

"The gold is his arms and legs; if I were as weak as he, I would hold on to it, too." It was Magnus the Fair. He was walking behind us and had overheard our conversation.

"You showed him no kindness when we were at the hall."

I could hear in Hakon's tone that he was still angry at Magnus.

"Many men are easier to pity when you are not in their company."

When Magnus finished speaking, I realized that I, too — now, when I could no longer see Hjalte or hear his whining voice, except in my memory — felt pity for him.

We had walked past Earl Hakon's hall and were

103

nearing the beach, not far from which our ship was anchored, when we heard someone running behind us. We all stopped and turned. Hjalte Gudbrandson's slave, the one his grandmother had called Sven, was coming towards us. When he saw us turn, he stopped running. He was out of breath and his forehead was wet with sweat.

The slave bowed several times to Hakon and smiled; then taking from his belt a little leather bag, he held it out to Hakon. Hakon opened the bag, looked into it, and passed it on to Rark and Erp the Traveler, who stood near him.

"Why are you giving me this money?"

The slave did not answer Hakon, but pointed in the direction of Hjalte's hall.

"Is your name Sven?"

The slave nodded his head and smiled, but did not speak.

"Why don't you answer?"

The slave stopped smiling. By pointing to his mouth and shaking his head, he made us understand that he was mute. None of us was surprised, for we had grown used to a strange world since the sun had risen that morning.

"Shall I keep it?" Hakon looked at the others. Rark looked away.

Erp the Traveler said, "Hjalte or his grandmother, Gudrun, must be afraid, since they are willing to pay blood money that no one has asked for."

Hakon, still looking doubtfully at the bag that Erp had passed back into his hands, said, "What evil story could these coins not tell?"

Rark made Hakon's decision for him. "I shall return to Hjalte's hall," he said, "and tell him that we wished no blood money for the slaying of Olaf Sigurdson. But we shall accept the money as a gift. And though we can never be friends, we shall do him no evil, but leave him to his fate."

Hakon nodded to the slave and put the bag in his own belt. The slave bowed again; first to Hakon, then to the rest of us; and quickly left us. Rark, walking slowly but determinedly, followed him. There was not one among us who did not admire Rark's willingness to return to Hjalte's hall; yet none offered to go with him.

When we had climbed down to the beach, Hakon spread out his cape upon the sand and emptied onto it all the coins from the bag. On Rogen, we were not used to money. We traded wares for wares; or as was the custom in older times, we used silver armbands as if they were coins.

Here there were twenty-two coins of different sizes, all of them of gold. I took the biggest one in my hand and looked at it. On one side was the picture of a strange man: some mighty king; on the other, that of a flower.

"What is the price of a man?" Magnus the Fair's voice came from above me, for I had been kneeling down, and he was standing behind me.

The statement had made Hakon angry and he started to gather up the coins. As I threw the big coin that I had held down on the cloak, Erp the Traveler said, "That one alone would buy a slave." Again I looked at the large coin. Hakon's fingers were picking it up, to throw it back into the bag.

"Well," I thought, "it is good to know one's value." Smiling bitterly, I turned, and walked down to the water's edge.

"But I am not a slave!" I said to myself. "But you were once," my heart answered; and my right hand picked up a stone, and threw it as far out to sea as I could.

15

I HAD BEGGED Hakon to allow me to stay on the ship when he and the others went to Earl Hakon's hall; but both he and Rark had been too frightened of the Earl to let me remain behind. "But I am afraid of the Earl and his slave," I had stammered.

"On the goodwill of the Earl depend not only our chances of buying a new sail and stores for our ship, but also our lives," Hakon had explained. "Earl Hakon's title is only Earl, but he is the ruler of all of Norway."

Again I washed myself and combed my hair; and again Gretha kindly loaned me her silver brooch.

"To Odin and to Thor, who rule our lives and set our courses!" Earl Hakon held high his golden cup, as if he wanted to show it off to the gods.

"To Odin and to Thor!" echoed the men around the table as they put their cups of mead to their lips. I sat at the lower end of the table among the less important guests and the members of Earl Hakon's hird who were either very old, or very young, or not well born.

"Three winters ago, half the men here forswore Odin and pledged their honor to the new god. They say that when Earl Hakon was in Denmark, he too forswore the old gods," the man mumbled who sat beside me. I turned to him. His face was furrowed. I knew he was called Leif the Noseless, a name he had received after a battle against King Eirik Bloodaxe. Leif had won much fame in his time. His body was covered with scars; and though his last scar was as honorably received as any of the others, it had brought him only ridicule and this mocking name.

"They say Magnus Thorsen was a believer in the new god," I remarked, for I was still thinking of Hjalte Gudbrandson and wanted the old man to talk about Magnus and his grandson.

"Magnus had only one god: gold! This is the most jealous of all gods. It creeps into the man who worships it and turns his heart and brain into metal."

I looked towards the far end of the long table at the many faces, and wondered if any of them worshiped any other gods but power and gold. A young man, sitting not far from Earl Hakon's seat, lifted his cup and spoke a verse. For a moment everyone was still, and I could hear the words plainly.

> "Empty the halls
> Of Jomcastle strong,
> Broken the walls,
> That stood so long.
> Bue's name
> The wind will tell,
> Earl Hakon's fame
> In hearts will dwell."

When the young man finished declaiming his verse, he held high his cup and said Earl Hakon's name, then he drank. Earl Hakon smiled to the young man, and turned to talk with Hakon Olafson, who sat at his side.

The old man bent towards me. He talked softly, but with a bitterness that spoke ill for the future of Earl Hakon if many men shared his opinions. "An ill-made verse, the poet's tongue is called flattery; his breath, envy; and his song, ambition. When Earl Hakon defeated Bue and his hird, they fought five against one; and rather would I have the wind tell my name than live in the heart of a coward."

"Is it not mostly in the sagas that battles are won by courage rather than numbers?"

My question seemed to embarrass the old man, for he looked down at the meat, which he held in his hand, and did not answer.

Not far from us, on the other side of the table, sat a young man who was looking angrily at the old man at my side. Leif the Noseless noticed that I had seen the young man. He shrugged his shoulders and whispered, "When a man gets so old that he can no longer wield the sword, he must learn to control his tongue. My son fears that I shall get both of us in trouble with the Earl." The old man took a drink of mead, stuffed some meat in his mouth, and tried to chew it.

Quiet, when unexpected, can come as such a surprise, that it frightens you, as a scream would. Such a stillness now came over the company. I looked up towards the high seat where the Earl sat and blushed, for

it appeared as if he and the men around him were staring at me.

"I bring news for you, Earl Hakon!"

The voice had come from behind me; and like everyone else, I looked to see who the speaker was. Standing near the doors of the entrance was a tall man. Though he was well dressed, his appearance spoke of a newly completed journey.

"Sit down, Ragne Ulvson. If you have been long at sea, you must know hunger for warm food."

The tall man made no movement to seat himself. "Long have I eaten only dried fish and dried meat; and long have I hoped to drink the Earl's mead, but the teller of misfortune seldom is a welcome guest."

The Earl frowned; and whereas frowning makes most men look sad, it made the Earl look frightening. "Not even to Odin is all news good. Tell us your tale, so we can get on with our meal."

The tall man glanced around the table, as if only now he had discovered that the Earl was not alone. "King Olaf Trygveson is on the Orkney Islands. Earl Sigurd Lodveson has forsworn the old gods, and is now King Olaf's man."

I did not know who Olaf Trygveson was, or what sea washed the sands of the Orkney Islands; but that the news was evil and unwelcome to the Earl, his face told me as plainly as words could have. He stood up, surveyed his guests; then nodding to Ragne Ulvson to follow him, he left the hall. When the Earl was gone, everyone spoke up at once, and I could make little sense of what was said. The old man beside me said —

111

not to me, but to himself — "Soon Odin's ravens masterless will be."

Since the Earl did not return; the men rose from the table and walked outside. The news had to be discussed and none was satisfied with only his neighbor's ear. No one talked to me. I was but a girl, and news of war was too important to waste on me. I was relieved when Hakon ordered all of us, except Erp the Traveler and Rark, to return to the ship. Magnus the Fair was as sour as milk four days old; he had enjoyed talking with the other men. On the way back to the beach, he would not speak to me. I walked alone, behind the others, thinking that King Olaf Trygveson — whoever he was — had done me a good deed, for I had feared that once the meal was over, Earl Hakon would remember me, and his slave, Kark, would recall the blow I had given him.

16

We were seven days in Tronhjem and the gods treated us kindly. The Earl sold Hakon a good sail, at a price even a miser would have called cheap. *Munin*'s old sail would never have lasted a storm. Since few ships had come to Tronhjem the winter before, skins were plentiful and not expensive.

On the fourth day after our visit to the Earl's hall, it was rumored that the Earl was leaving Tronhjem to take part in a feast, held at Medalhus, in Gauldal. Near noon of that day the Earl, with ten men from his hird and two women from his hall, came to the beach, near where *Munin* was anchored, to bid Hakon farewell. We had been busy sorting and bundling skins for storage on board the ship; but on the arrival of the guests, we all stopped work.

The men of Earl Hakon's hird were all strong and fine-looking, but none of them was very tall. It was told that Earl Hakon, being of ordinary height himself, did not like men who were too tall about him. The Earl was dressed plainly, as he had been when we had been his guests the first time; but his cape was held together by two gold snakes, whose tails could be locked into each other.

Hakon had a barrel of the best mead brought from *Munin.* We women served the guests and those of the crew for whom there were cups, for we had brought from Rogen only one cup to each man on board. The news of Olaf Trygveson being on the Orkney Islands no longer seemed to bother the Earl. He joked with Hakon, saying that if he were younger, he would sail with him; for to drink mead such as ours, any man would gladly take his turn at the oars. Hakon returned the compliment, and said that he would gladly sail *Munin* in the Earl's fleet, should Earl Hakon need him. Although I had kept myself far away from the Earl and his slave, Kark, who attended him, I could hear what was said; and I could not help looking at Hakon when he offered to serve the Earl, for I knew he cared little for his famous kinsman.

Hakon ordered more mead to be given to our guests. Rigmor Ragnvaldsdaughter took a wooden pitcher, filled it up, and poured some of it into the Earl's cup. The Earl was as famous for his many love affairs and his many wives as he was for his courage. It was said that one of the reasons that he did not like the new religion was that it forbids a man to have more than one wife. When Rigmor had poured the mead, he grabbed her around the waist and laughingly said, "My cousin, like the gods, keeps beautiful women about him, even when he is on a journey. Are they all so fair on Rogen as these? How many do you have along?"

Before Hakon could answer, Rigmor grinned and said, "The Earl must visit Rogen and see for himself. We are four on board."

"Five," Hakon snapped, "and not all equally well be-haved."

The Earl raised his eyebrows and looked at Rigmor, who stared back at him boldly and said, "Only four of us are freeborn."

I turned to run away when a woman's voice said, "Freeborn are only those who have not the worm of envy gnawing at their hearts." The speaker was Thora of Remul, a woman of great beauty and wealth, of whom it was said the Earl was very fond.

"In that case, Rigmor has her father's soul, and I fear she has no heart at all," said Hakon and looked so an-grily at Rigmor that she became frightened and turned pale.

"To keep order among women is as difficult as mak-ing hens stop pecking each other," said Earl Hakon and laughed.

"Or as difficult as keeping a cock from crowing," added Thora Remul. For as always happens when a man mixes in a fight among women, the women turn against him. Thora of Remul now looked scornfully at the Earl, turned her back and started walking in the direction of the Earl's hall. I watched her as she de-parted; and thanking her silently, I thought: What a beautiful name Thora is. Now I know two women bear-ing that name who have been kind to me.

The Earl gave Hakon a gold arm ring, explaining that it had belonged to Hakon's great-grandfather; then he and his men bade us farewell. As soon as they were gone, Hakon turned to Rigmor; but luckily for her, the ring had taken the sharp edge from his anger.

Poor Rigmor's spite had been more evil than she had intended it: she knew only that I had slapped Earl Hakon's slave, Kark; no one, I am sure, had told her of the Earl's jest, that if I had been a slave, he would have bought me and married me to Kark.

"Your father was a traitor," Hakon began. "This I have forgiven him; and I would not hold it against you if you did not pride yourself on your birth. That you were born free is the gift of the gods and your parents' luck. It gives you neither honor nor dishonor. What you become, this alone shall you be judged by."

Rigmor opened her mouth to say something, to defend herself against Hakon's words; but he raised his hand — a signal that he would not have her speak.

"You have dishonored yourself, by trying to bring shame on one of your comrades. You are a grown woman, but have behaved as a child who tells lies about his playfellows to get the attention of the grownups. You deserve that I cut a switch and beat you, as one would a naughty child. Go, finish your work; and behave in the future in a manner so that I shall not notice you."

Rigmor's face had been pale while Hakon had been speaking, until he called her a child and said she deserved to be switched; then it grew red like blood. Many of the men laughed. Rigmor began to weep and her dignity was gone. I wished that they had not laughed, for justice is a bird that flies away when people take pleasure in others' pain.

The day after the Earl left Tronhjem, *Munin* was

loaded; and we were ready to sail; but we had to wait yet another day and night before we could depart. The day following our arrival in Tronhjem, Hakon had sent Nils, the younger son of Harold the Bowbender, on horseback, south to the hall of Ulv Erikson to seek news of Hakon's stepmother, Thora Magnusdaughter, and my mother, Gunhild. The last day in Tronhjem was spent waiting for Nils and for Gunhild; that is, if Gunhild was living at Ulv's hall and Nils could persuade Ulv to sell her.

The thought of seeing my mother again made me restless. Hakon sensed my unhappiness. He came up to me while I was walking aimlessly along the beach, and said, "I gave Nils enough gold to buy a young slave. I gave him two of the bigger coins that were in the bag Hjalte Gudbrandson sent his slave, Sven, to give me. Surely, Ulv could not ask more for Gunhild." Hakon put his hand on my shoulder and forced me to stand still. "It is because he has her with him that Nils is taking so long."

For a moment, I wanted to tell Hakon the truth: that I feared the coming of my mother would make me a slave again; but looking into his eyes, I realized that I could not. Though Hakon's hand rested near my cheek, I felt miserably alone.

"Do you think she can endure a journey like ours?" I asked, because the silence seemed so heavy.

My question made Hakon smile. "She is not that old."

Suddenly I realized that to me, my mother had always been old; and it was a shock to admit that what

Hakon said was true. She had only been sixteen winters old when she had given birth to me.

"You were too hard on Rigmor," I said.

"Not half as hard as she deserved." Then he laughed and added, "Rark and Magnus have laughed much at the thought of me switching Rigmor. To tell the truth — though I meant it, when I said it — I don't think, now, that I could have done it."

I sat down on the sand. Looking up at Hakon, I too laughed, for I found it as impossible as everyone else to imagine him with a stick in hand, hitting Rigmor.

"By the Gods, I would have done it!" he said and flung himself down next to me on the warm sand. "I dislike people who pick their pride from their ancestors' graves."

Hakon's face was turned towards me. I knew he meant what he said: he, who could count so many of the famous heroes of Norway as his kin! The thought came to me: And you, Helga, are afraid of your mother coming, for you are ashamed of the one who has borne you.

I scooped up a handful of sand. "But Rigmor has never learned anything but pride," I said to Hakon; and added silently, to myself: And I, nothing but shame.

Hakon looked up at the sky and the sun, which shone brightly; then he lowered his head and sighed. "Oh, Helga, I am not as clever as you are: I see only the storm when it comes, but you have seen from where the winds gather."

"To love another is freedom for yourself," I thought. "To love only yourself is like being your own

118

slave." And then, for that short time that I sat with Hakon on the beach, I forgave all who had ever hurt me, and I felt certain that no one could ever harm me again.

Nils Haroldson returned early the next morning. We were sleeping on board, and I was awakened by the noise the watchmen made when they were getting the small boat ready to row to the beach to fetch Nils. With sleep-filled eyes, I got up and looked toward the shore. Nils was alone; my mother had not come with him. I looked about for Hakon, intending to wake him, but he was already standing at the railing waiting for the small boat to return. Stepping carefully over the sleeping men, I joined him.

When he saw me he smiled and whispered, "Don't worry, little sister. I had a dream that no harm had come to Gunhild."

As soon as the boat came alongside, Hakon shouted to Nils, "Is Gunhild alive?"

Nils nodded and looked at me happily.

"How is Thora Magnusdaughter?" I asked as he swung himself on board.

"Better ask how fares Ulv Hunger. That wolf found his mate in sheep's clothing when he married Thora," he said and grinned broadly. "I bring greetings from Thora and from Gunhild. They are both as well as one can fare while living under the same roof as Ulv Hunger," he said and laughed.

"But you did not bring Gunhild. Would Ulv not sell her?"

This question made Nils laugh so hard that it was a while before he could answer. "I think Ulv would have sold you both Thora and Gunhild for the price of a rotten fish. But he could sell neither, for Thora is his wife, and Gunhild's freedom Thora bought as part of the marriage agreement. I could have brought Ulv Hunger as part of the crew, for he would gladly put the sea between himself and his hall."

By now most of the men were awake and they crowded around Nils Haroldson to hear his story. With much laughter and merriment, Nils told of how Ulv Erikson had in Thora gotten a master, not a wife. "She rules his hall, for all his men listen to her; and though Ulv sits in the high seat at table, he hardly dares order his cup filled with mead." As for Gunhild, my mother, she said she would rather become a slave again than venture out on a sea journey like ours. Thora had sent with Nils three gold rings and the silver armbands, which were part of the treasure that Ulv Erikson had stolen when he had visited us on Rogen.

All of the men were in excellent spirits and praised Hakon's luck: how he had gotten both revenge over his enemy and part of his inheritance back, without having to lift his sword. One of the old men said that such was Hakon's good fortune that one would think he had Odin as a foster-father. Erp the Traveler said that from now on, we should call Hakon Olafson Hakon the Lucky.

After we had eaten our morning meal, each man was given a cup of the best mead, to toast the success of our journey.

"Anchor up!" I heard Hakon call, and when I leaned out over the railing and looked into the water, I saw that the ship was moving.

"Oars ready!" I looked towards land. In the distance, I could see the roof of the Earl's great hall. When will we be back? I thought, while in my ears I heard the men cry, "Anchor is up!"

"Row!" Hakon shouted. At the noise of the oars entering the water, I turned and looked out towards the fjord and the great sea beyond it.

17

AT THE END of the first day, we had only reached the entrance to the fjord; for the wind had been westerly, and we had had to row all the way. We anchored for the first night in the lee of a small island, where we collected driftwood and cooked our supper. The following day, the wind shifted to the north. We set sail. Our course was close to the mainland, in that sound which separates Norway from the large island called Hitra. At midday, when we had reached the southern tip of the island, the man who was on watch at *Munin*'s bow cried out that he had sighted ships coming against us.

We leapt from our places and stared ahead. I could see some black dots on that line where water and sky join each other. We did not alter course, and soon we saw that they were five longships. They were being rowed and were coming directly against us.

"Those ships carry a message not welcome to Earl Hakon, for I believe they come from the Orkney Islands, and their leader is King Olaf Trygveson," said Erp the Traveler after he stood long, staring at the approaching ships.

"What message do they carry for us?" asked Hakon, looking grimly ahead.

"A message we had better not receive," answered Erp, and looked up at the sail.

"Can they outsail us, if they should care to pursue us?" Rark asked.

"Outrow us, they can; for their smallest ship has at least fifty oars. But they are even heavier loaded than we are, and do not have their sails up."

For a moment all three of them stood silent, gazing at the oncoming fleet. "Shouldn't we change course?" Rark demanded. Erp the Traveler only shook his head.

Now that we could plainly see the ships, we knew that what Erp had said was true: the smallest of them was at least twice the size of *Munin*. They were lying low in the water and carried many men. Four of the boats had dragons' heads mounted in their bows; the fifth, the largest of the ships, had a cross, the symbol of the new god.

"I shall change course so that we pass west of them; but I shall not do it before we are so close to them that it will come as a surprise," Erp said to Hakon, and walked aft to take the steering oar himself.

"Let each man take his shield, so that he can protect himself should they shoot arrows at us. But let no one shoot back." At Hakon's order, the shields were taken from where they were stored and given to their owners. I had no shield. When Hakon noticed this, he motioned to Ketil Ragnvaldson to protect me with his.

The wind was blowing strongly now, and the timber

of *Munin* was groaning as she moved through the water.

"Prepare to alter course!" shouted Erp.

Four men loosened the ropes of the sail, so that it could be turned to catch the wind on our new course.

"Pull!" Erp screamed.

The big sail was pulled farther towards midship. *Munin* heeled over as she changed course, and the wind hit her almost sideways. I felt the deck rise beneath me. My feet slipped and I tumbled down towards the port railing. Ketil Ragnvaldson caught hold of my shoulder and held me.

I had lain on the deck only a moment, yet I had seen

the ship that passed nearest us. Some of the men seemed to be shouting to us; but I hardly noticed them — or the men who were rowing — for my attention was given to the two men standing midship with their arrows resting on their drawn bowstrings. I felt that both of their arrows were pointed at me, and the thought made it impossible for me to move. Had not Ketil pulled at my shoulder, I think I would have remained lying there on the deck, a perfect target.

"Prepare to change course!" Erp called out again. The men pulled on the ropes. *Munin* was back on her old course, to the south, with the wind directly aft.

The two men had shot their arrows, not at me but at the steersman. They had missed. Erp appeared unconcerned, though one of the arrows was embedded in the railing, not half of a spear's length way from where he stood. As soon as we were well past the foreign ships, we came out of our hiding places behind the shields.

The men on board the other ships had stopped rowing; obviously they were waiting for orders from the big ship with a cross in its bow.

"If they don't make up their minds soon, they'll have a difficult race!" shouted Hakon the Black triumphantly as the distance between *Munin* and the strangers' ships became greater and greater.

We heard the sound of orders being shouted, but we were too far away to understand them. A moment later, the movements of the ships told us what the orders had been: the four largest ships kept their course north, but the fifth turned and sailed in our direction. It took the men of this ship some time to hoist their sail;

and although they kept rowing while the sail was being gotten ready, they lost distance. When finally their sail was up and they could pull in their oars, we were so far away from them that we could no longer see the faces of the men on board.

Since I was standing beside Ketil Ragnvaldson, I turned to him and asked the question to which every man on board *Munin* would have liked to know the answer: "Will they outsail us?"

Ketil shook his head and said, "Their ship is more broadly built and more heavily loaded than *Munin*; but if the biggest ship had turned, we would have little chance of escape."

My relief gave me courage to ask the next question: "If they caught up with us, what would they do?"

Ketil pulled at his hair and grinned. "Oh, they would kill us: men, women, and child."

The "child," I knew, had been added to tease me; and I frowned at Ketil to show my annoyance.

"I am sorry that my sister, Rigmor, hurt you, Helga."

I looked up at Ketil to see whether he was serious, or if this was merely a new way of teasing me. Ketil looked back at me with such concern that I forgot my suspicions and began thinking how different he was from his sister.

"I just wish she did not hate me," I explained. "I mean her no harm."

Ketil sighed. "Those people who hate much, seldom need reasons for it."

Ketil's remark gave me little hope of ever becoming

126

friends with Rigmor. But to be truthful, I did not want to be her friend; what I wanted was that she should not be my enemy.

A great cry went up from the crew of *Munin*. I looked aft, towards our pursuer. The ship had pulled down its sail; it was giving up the chase.

"Well, now you will never know what they would have done to us," Ketil said and smiled.

"Ah, but they could not have caught us, anyway. A very wise and old man told me so."

Ketil laughed. "Oh, he was neither old nor wise; but certainly he is much relieved at being shown to be right."

I glanced at the faces of the men about me, and realized that Ketil was not the only man whose fear had left him when our pursuers had taken down their sail.

"But we have done those people no harm."

Ketil looked at me thoughtfully. "No," he said, "we have done them no harm; neither have you done Rigmor any harm, nor has the rabbit done the hungry fox any harm."

There were many other things I wanted to know. I looked about for Hakon; but he was talking with Erp the Traveler and I dared not approach them.

That night we anchored on North More, at a place called Vevang. It has its name from the God Ve, who was one of the brothers of Odin, and had helped Odin create the world out of the body of the Giant Ymer.

Here the land was low and grassy. Some of the men went hunting for birds while others fished; but neither the fishermen nor the hunters had any luck, and we roasted a sheep for our dinner. After we had eaten, most of the men retired to the ship; but I did not want to return to the cramped quarters aboard *Munin*.

Among the grass grew many flowers. I picked a lot of yellow ones and braided them into a garland, as I had done so many times on Rogen. So busy was I braiding the flowers that I did not notice that someone was standing watching me until I heard him cough.

"Hakon," I said and raised my head.

It was Magnus the Fair; and I realized that he must have been smiling, and that when I had mistakenly called Hakon's name, his smile had faded. "The garlands of victory," he said, neither sadly nor gaily.

I shook my head. "They are just the garlands of spring . . . of summer . . . or maybe of my childhood."

"Hakon the Lucky," he almost shouted and sat down beside me. He picked up the garland that I had just finished making.

"Ketil said that if they had caught us, they would have killed us. Do you think that is right?"

Magnus pursed his lips. "Ketil is young. He likes to think that he has been in more danger than he has."

I laughed, remembering that Ketil had told me that I was a child, for Magnus was only four or five winters older than Ketil.

"The new god seems to like the sound of battle as much as Odin does," I said.

Magnus put the garland that he was holding in his hands around my neck. "The gods are what you make

128

of them. Who knows the will of the gods? From what I have heard of the new god, he believes that men should live in poverty; yet his followers have crooked backs from picking up gold. He wore no sword either, but his followers, like King Olaf Trygveson, seem to want to preach his message with an army." He spoke more softly: "But I am eager to learn of this new god, for Odin and Thor do not satisfy me. I am not a coward, nor do I fear death; but brutality is not courage."

Magnus stopped talking a moment and picked a flower that grew near where he was sitting. He started tearing the leaves from it. "Do you, Helga, believe in Odin?"

I thought for a while, as I watched Magnus' fingers tear the flower apart. It had never occurred to me before, not to believe. "During the long winter nights, especially when the north wind blows, I know I do believe. But I have never thought of Odin as my friend, in the way Hakon's father, Olaf Sigurdson, did. But I was once a slave, and Odin cares little for slaves."

Magnus the Fair threw away the bare stem of the flower, and looked out over the sea. "Fear preaches well the power of the gods. They say the new god does not allow his worshipers to own slaves."

I had finished my second garland and was putting it down beside me. "Then I shall believe in the new god," I said and smiled up at Magnus.

Magnus picked up the garland and hung it on top of the other one, around my neck. "And I shall worship only you, Helga!"

I frowned. Although Magnus' words did not displease me, they worried me. He misunderstood and thought I was angry. "Many servants are not freer than slaves," he said seriously.

Suddenly I was angry. "That is not true! A slavish servant has had a choice: his slavery is his own fault; but a man or a woman that is born a slave is born a cripple!"

Magnus laughed at my earnestness. "Ah, but some cripples are born with awfully straight limbs, and have little difficulty outrunning the freeborn."

I laughed too; but at the same time, I was realizing that the freeborn — even Magnus! — would never understand the slave.

"What stories is Magnus telling you, that you laugh so freely?"

I looked up. Hakon was standing behind me, trying very hard to smile pleasantly at Magnus and me.

"Sit down, Hakon the Lucky. We are discussing weighty problems, such as how can a one-eyed god like Odin see the whole world at once?"

Hakon sat down beside Magnus. The sight of them both opposite me, looking so serious, made me laugh. I took my two garlands and threw one on each pair of shoulders. Both Hakon and Magnus smiled; but, flower garlanded as they were, they looked uncomfortably at each other.

In the distance, a great rock protruded from the meadow. As I started running, I called out, "Let's race to the rock!"

I ran as fast as I could. Behind me, I could hear Magnus and Hakon running. As I neared the rock,

Hakon passed me; then, touching the rock, he turned a triumphant face back at me. Magnus reached the rock only a moment after I did.

We fell exhausted on the grass; and then because we were young and tired, and soon it would be summer — when the sky of the north has no night — we started to laugh, all three of us.

18

TWO DAYS LATER, we camped for the last time on the soil of Norway; and many days would go by before we again would taste warm food. The last sight of our homeland was a barren peninsula called Stad. Here in a cove we built a fire and Hakon ordered a double portion of mead to be given to everyone. But most of us were thinking of Rogen; we felt a little sad and the meal was not gay. Even when Orm, one of the older men who told stories well, started to tell the tale of Hagbart and Signe, which was a favorite of us all, our attention wandered.

When Orm came to the part of the story where Signe burns herself to death in her house because her father has killed Hagbart whom she loved, Astrid Erpsdaughter laughed and said, "That poet knew little about women, for no woman would kill herself by burning, for fear the fire would make her ugly."

Erp, who was a great lover of the tales — though he could not tell them well himself — angrily bid his daughter be quiet, so Orm could finish his tale.

I agreed with Astrid that Signe chose a death that was too horrible. Although fire is our friend, it is also our enemy; and all of us have felt the pain of a burn often enough not to want to embrace it. When Orm ended the story, with Signe's father's repentance after he hears of his daughter's death, we went on board, to sleep.

When the sun rose, Hakon woke us. After a meal of bread and water, the sail was hoisted and *Munin* sailed out towards the open sea. We all watched the barren rocky coast as it disappeared, as if our eyes feared looking forward, towards the endless sea.

I was lying with some skins covering me on the deck, looking at the mast of *Munin*. It was the evening of our third day without sight of land. The wind was still blowing from the north and *Munin* had both wind and waves coming directly aft. She rolled from side to side as she slid down the big waves. Rising to the top of each new wave, her bow pointing skyward, she shivered before she again ran down the back of a wave to bury herself in foam. The sky was clear; in the west, it was still bloody from the setting sun.

I had been retelling myself the story of Gudrun and Sigurd, and the Valkyrie Brynhild. I was thinking that although both Gudrun and Brynhild had been beautiful and clever women, they had not been loved by either Sigurd or Gunner. For Sigurd had loved the golden treasure that he had taken from the snake Fafner (after he had killed it), far more than he had ever loved either Gudrun or Brynhild. And Gunner had only loved Brynhild because she was a Valkyrie and knew Odin. "If Brynhild had been a slave," I thought, "neither Sigurd nor Gunner would ever have noticed her." I yawned and closed my eyes.

All of a sudden, I heard the sound as of the bough of a tree breaking. I had almost been asleep. Although I did not know from whence the noise had come, I looked up at the sail. The heavy rope that the sail was hauled up by was broken. The big spar, made of heavy timber, that held the sail outstretched, was now held by two smaller — much thinner — ropes.

I threw off the skins that covered me; but before I could get up, the two ropes burst. The spar and the sail fell with a great crash down upon the deck. The sail fell on top of me and threw me back onto the deck, but the spar did not hit me.

I had fallen headfirst, and hit my face against the deck so hard that my nose began to bleed. There was panic on board *Munin*, and no one noticed me as I crawled out from under the sail.

"Put out the aft oars and row!" screamed Erp the Traveler as he pushed the steering oar toward port, to prevent the ship from lying sideways against the waves.

"Haul in the spar!" Hakon shouted, for the spar had smashed the port railing and was trailing in the water, making it impossible for Erp to steer.

I was still half kneeling on the deck when I found that my hand was holding on to one of the oars that had been stacked in a row, midship. I picked the oar up. It was heavy, but I managed to drag it over to one of the holes. I removed the piece of wood that closed the oar hole when the ship was under sail and slid the oar through the hole.

Many times had I rowed small boats; but on Rogen I only went out when the sea was still, and the oars of small boats are light. Now as I bent my back forward to pull the oar through the water, the water disappeared and I almost fell over backward. Then when I should have pushed the oar through the air, the force of a wave that broke against *Munin*'s side nearly twisted it out of my hand. I was being drenched by the spray from the wave when two hands grabbed me from behind and threw me midship, while Ketil Ragnvaldson took hold of the oar.

We had seen the finger of the sea. Had we felt its hand, then *Munin* would have become driftwood for others to cook their meals over; and we, food for those giant snakes that live on the sunless land below the waves. Nonetheless, the sea had demanded a sacrifice and taken from us one man. Reimer Eigilson was his name. The spar, when it fell, had hit him and thrown him overboard; then a wave had covered him and he was gone. He had been a quiet man and well liked; married but three winters, he had a baby son on Rogen, to whom Hakon was godfather.

New ropes were taken from their storage place, cut, and fastened; soon the sail was raised once more. Few slept that night. We talked about Reimer, finding in recalling some words he had said, or some action he had done, comfort from our own fears.

Nine times the sun rose in the east and set in the west, while *Munin* kept her course south. On the ninth day, in the evening, Erp the Traveler gave orders to change course, west towards where the sun had set. The wind was northwest; the sail had to be pulled down and the men ordered to the oars. None of them was sorry, for we had grown stiff from the cramped quarters on deck.

It seemed to me a wonder how Erp the Traveler knew when to change the course of the ship. The sea has no mountains to guide one; it looks alike in north or south; and any path across it seems equally purposeful. We were all a little frightened of Erp. He was the oldest of the crew and had traveled to many strange lands. It was, therefore, with some fear that I asked him how he could tell where we were, and if the gods whispered it to him while he slept.

Erp was in good humor. Had he not been, he would merely have scowled or laughed at me. "See that star?" he said and pointed a finger towards the sky.

As we sailed south, there were more and more stars to be seen in the summer sky; and though I said yes, I was not sure which star Erp meant.

"That star some men call Odin's Eye; and others call it the North Star. When Odin, Vile, and Ve created the heavens, out of the skull of the Giant Ymer, they set sparks upon it, from the fire of Muspellsheim. Some of the sparks were allowed to fly around in circles, but others were fastened to the heavens to guide men across the seas. Of all the stars that guide men, the North Star is the best friend of seamen, for it does not move; therefore, it has been called Odin's Eye, for truly like an eye, we can see by it."

Erp took from his tunic a piece of leather string,

which had been knotted in many places. "See here, child." He held up the string at an arm's distance in front of us, so that the end of it was level with that line where the sea and sky meet. "When the North Star is blotted out by the third knot, then it is time to turn on a western course, if we wish to sail through the sound that separates England from that land our forefathers called Walland, and we now call Frankland. Frankland is a large country, which stretches from one sea southward to another. The father of my father's father was a member of Rolf the Wanderer's hird when he conquered it." Erp put away his string and looked with longing towards the south, as if his eyes could see the great chief, Rolf, and his men.

I looked up at the stars, but all seemed alike to me. How could those sparks which Odin set upon the sky still be burning? I thought. I dared not ask Erp, for he was a strong believer in the old gods, and he might think I was making a jest about them.

The night was warm, much warmer than any night I had ever known on Rogen. The wind had almost died down. I walked to my sleeping place. Before I fell asleep I cast one last glance at the sky and the stars, which Erp could read as others could read the Runic letters.

19

AFTER SAILING four days and four nights on a western course, on the morning of the fifth day — that is, sixteen days after we had set sail from Tronhjem — we saw land. We were overjoyed and wanted to head the ship for the shore at once. But Erp said it was the coast of England and we would find no friends there. Yet the wish of the crew for feeling the earth under their feet was so great that Hakon thought it wiser to allow a landing.

The coastline was low and marshy. About an arrow's flight from shore, the sea was so shallow that we anchored. Most of the men could not wait to be rowed ashore in the little boat, so holding their weapons above their heads, they waded through the water, which was not quite waist-deep. I came ashore in the boat with the other women, and the cooking pots. Rigmor Ragnvaldsdaughter sat in the stern while I sat in the bow. Since the incident in Tronhjem, we had not spoken to each other.

It was strange walking on land again, for the land seemed to move under me as the deck of *Munin* had done. When the men had waded ashore, some ducks had taken to their wings; soon almost all of the men were hunting. Erp grumbled, and kept calling to the men not to go too far away from where the ship was anchored, and not to go anywhere alone.

"In this part of England live many Danes. They are not to be trusted. Denmark is low and flat. It has no mountains to make a man's heart beat with pride. At table, they eat like pigs and drink like hogs. Their poets are flatterers."

Erp's words made Hakon laugh. But Erp wrinkled his brow and looked fiercely out over the marshland. "Remember Sven the Dane," he said bitterly, "wasn't he the worst of the traitors?"

When Erp named Sven the Dane, I remembered how Ragnvald Harelip had killed Sven while he was begging Hakon for his life.

"Even to the gods, the Danes are treacherous. King Gorm bargained with Odin and the new god, as if he were buying a horse. Trust not the smile of a Dane, Hakon, for it covers an unsmiling heart."

Hakon looked out at *Munin*, which was lying quietly at anchor. "There are many Danes. One must not judge all of them from the behavior of one man, or even a king. Still, we shall not spend the night, but sail after we have eaten."

Erp kicked angrily at the ground. "I would rather be among the Franks . . . And you are wrong, for one can judge a bird by its nest."

I thought much about what Erp had said, but I could not agree with him. Surely, I would not like to be judged by the behavior of Earl Hakon or Hjalte Gudbrandson. But most men who see well the faults of strange peoples walk as if they were blind when they are at home.

We met no Danes, but we did have a feast. The men had shot so many ducks that there was more than one for each of us. Though duck is best when it is not freshly killed, the plain fare that we had eaten for so many days on *Munin* sharpened our teeth. We emptied the last of the barrels of mead. The thought of soon tasting the drink of the Franks, which is called wine, and in the north is only drunk by kings and earls, made everyone excited; and we greeted the emptiness of the barrel as a good omen.

The sun was about to set when we returned to *Munin*. The men were tired and no one wanted to row. But Erp the Traveler would not allow us to anchor so close to the shore. *Munin* was rowed away from land until the coastline, in the twilight, could only dimly be seen. Then we hoisted the sail, but the wind was less than a breeze, and *Munin* drifted more than she sailed. We were all too excited — and a little proud of ourselves — for having made a landing on foreign soil; and despite our weariness, no one could sleep.

The next day, the wind blew from the northwest. We followed the coastline south, until in the late afternoon it fell away. Erp told us that this was the fjord that formed the entrance to a river so broad that ships could sail up it for several days, until they came to a great town.

The following morning we sighted land again. By noon, we rounded the tip of England, where the sea is narrowest between England and Frankland. Erp told us that the coast here was formed of white chalk cliffs. We did not see them, for the wind was blowing very strongly and the rain coming down heavily. It was a westerly wind and the men had to row, for our course was southwest. The men at the oars cursed bitterly, for the waves were short, whitecapped, and difficult to row against; but I almost envied those who were rowing, for at least they were working and were not as cold as the rest of us. All that day, that night, and the next day, the weather was so bad that the men rowed with numb hands.

The evening of the second day, after we had passed the southern tip of England, the sky cleared and the stars came out. When next the sun rose, we expected to see land; and all except Erp the Traveler were bitterly disappointed when our eyes beheld the seemingly unending sea. Erp was undisturbed. He looked at the upcoming sun and changed our course to a more southern one. By noon the sun was bright, and all our clothes were dry. The wind had shifted. It came now from the northwest and we could hoist the sail again. At eve, just when the sun was setting, we saw land to the south.

"That is Frankland," said Erp.

All of us stared at the dim blue line that rose above the sea. I stood at the railing, my expectations belied: Frankland had no mountains like Norway.

Next to me were Rark and Hakon. "The nearness of my home frightens me. Perhaps I should never have come." Rark looked intently at the land; both his hands gripped tightly the railing.

"But your wife and children," Hakon mumbled

"Twelve times harvest has followed the spring thaw since last I saw my children. In my mind's eye, my boy is still four winters old, and my daughter, three. Somewhere in that land — if God has not taken their souls up to Him — live a young man and a young woman, in whose memory I can have only a very small part."

On Hakon's face, one could see that he wanted to comfort Rark, and that he did not know how. "The tears of an orphan are heavy like the icicles in the mountains, and love cannot melt them."

I felt in Hakon's words a bitterness that wounded me.

"Twelve winters have I dreamed, and now I need but count days before I must wake. I have prayed to my god, that he should protect my wife and children; but it is a long time since I have been in his house, and who knows if he has heard my prayers."

"Ship to starboard!" the watchman cried. All of us turned to see the sighted ship. It was smaller than *Munin*. Coming from the north and sailing south, it would cross *Munin*'s course. As we approached it, we realized that it was only a fishing boat; and there were only eight men on board.

"Pull down your sail!" Hakon shouted. Instead of obeying Hakon's order, the fishermen put out their oars and started to row, for the wind was very slight and they were not making much headway, since their sail was old and small.

From beside me, Rark shouted something. At once, the fishermen stopped rowing and started to pull down their sail.

"Rark spoke the language of Frankland to them!" I thought excitedly, remembering the strange, soft words I had heard him mutter in his sleep, when he was recovering from his wound after he had defeated Hakon's uncle.

We steered *Munin* up beside the fishing boat. With a rope, the two ships were tied together. Their leader was ordered on board our ship; and Rark, Erp, and Hakon met him in the stern of *Munin*.

The rest of us stood at the railing looking at the strange boat and its crew. They looked very frightened. One of them — an older man — kept making that sign with his fingers in front of him, which the believers in the new god use when they want to ward off evil. Their dress was poor. The nets, which lay in the stern of their boat, were thin and patched in many places. Beneath the nets, we could see their catch; there were but few fish, and they were small. Soon their leader was allowed to return to his boat, and we cast off the rope and let them sail on. The old man kept smiling to us, as if he had received a precious gift.

Rark had learned little from the fisherman. He had complained that fishing was bad and that the harvest, the autumn before, had been poor. But he was very frightened and would not have bragged. He did tell Rark that this part of Frankland (which is known as Normandy) was ruled by Duke Richard the Second. (Duke Richard the Second was the great-grandson of the mighty Viking, Walking Rolf, whose father had been Earl Ragnvald, friend of King Harold Fairhair, the famous King of Norway.)

143

Erp had asked Rark to find out if the Norsemen of Normandy were still faithful to the old gods. The fisherman had replied that all the people of Normandy were Christians, this being the name which the believers in the new god call themselves. Erp had grunted when Rark told him the man's answer. A moment later, he had asked Rark to find out whether a chieftain named Thormod still lived. The man had shaken his head and said that it was a long time since that Thormod had been killed. The fisherman, himself, who was a young man, remembered having heard of Thormod's death when he was a child. When Rark had explained what he had learned to Erp, Erp had walked away, as if he wished to hear no more of the state of affairs in Normandy.

By morning, when the sun came out of the sea, we had not only land to the south of us, but forward to the west, as well. This was a great cape, that we had to round. Erp altered course, keeping far away from land, since the currents and the tides around Normandy are treacherous, especially when the fog, which Norsemen call Loki's cape, comes rolling in from the sea.

We passed the tip of the cape at evening. The wind had died down, and the men were rowing again. The current was against us and we made little headway. Still, our spirit was high, for it was a warm night. Erp promised us that we would land the following day on one of the islands that he knew we would pass.

20

For a long time I have told of the shifting of winds, of sails and oars; and yet I do not believe that I have described our sea journey well. Once sail is hoisted and land is out of sight, man is dwarfed by his own courage that has removed him from the hearth of his home. Cold and wet is the sailor, lonely amidst his comrades, for the waves beat not only on the hull of the ship, but against his heart. When the ship is beached, men may boast of the storm; but while his country is the never ending sea and his house a tiny nutshell, he will speak softly of the gods.

When we landed on the island on which Erp had promised us we should guest, we felt that this was the end of our journey. We were in Frankland: from Rogen in the north we had sailed and outwitted the sea. Not that we saw much worth recounting on that island, or stayed very long. Already the morning after our landing, we put to sea again. We saw no inhabitants, though we since have been told that a Norseman was chieftain. Yet it was a symbol, a sign of our accomplishment; and though we knew that the island must have had another name, we called it "Hakon's Luck."

From "Hakon's Luck," we steered for the Island of Saint Michel, a place dedicated to one of the Christians' lesser gods, named Michel. Michel was the mightiest warrior in the new god's hird. It was Rark's idea that we should sail there first, so that we might learn news of Rark's family from the priest of the new god, who lived there.

It was almost evening and the tide was high when we came to the Island of Saint Michel, which was situated very near the mainland. It was a small and rocky island. Near its summit were a large stone building and a few small ones. Farther out to sea was a tiny island. It did not have an almost mountainlike peak as did the Island of Saint Michel, but only a low hill. No one lived on this small island and here we beached *Munin*.

When I was supposed to be collecting firewood, I climbed the hill in the middle of our island. I looked towards the mainland, which stretched low and marshy, as far as I could see. "Desolate," I thought. "Strange and foreign," I said aloud. Saint Michel's Island seemed out of place: rocky and steep, like a tiny Rogen that had set sail from Norway and anchored up here.

I saw light coming from the large building. This I could not understand, for I did not know then about glass: that material which can let the light pass through it; yet keeps the wind and rain out. I heard the soft sound of singing; and as the sun set, someone on the island rang a bell. It frightened me, and I ran down to the beach, where the fire for cooking our meal had already been lighted.

When the sun rose, we again heard the bell ring from the Island of Saint Michel. But this time we hardly noticed it; for we were staring in amazement at the sight of our own island. It had grown so much during the night that the beach, on which we had had just enough space to draw up *Munin*, now was broad enough to make our ship seem small. It was still wet from the retreating sea. We had known that the tide was strong, for the men had rowed against it; but that it could swallow up half the land of this island each day, and then like a great monster, vomit it up again each night, was the most astonishing thing that any of us had ever seen.

Hakon ordered the men to take lines and hooks, that we might have a hot fish soup for our midday meal.

By the time we finished eating, the tide had come in again, and our island was the same size as it had been when we found it.

Hakon, Rark, and four of the younger men, all armed, took the little boat and rowed to the Island of Saint Michel. The rest of us spent the afternoon fishing and swimming. The water was warmer than we had ever known it, even on the warmest day of summer on Rogen. By midafternoon, when the sea again was swiftly retreating, I began to be worried, for Hakon and Rark and their companions had not returned.

I climbed to the top of the hill, where I had been the day before. I looked towards the Island of Saint Michel. I saw our boat lying on the beach, many boat lengths from the sea.

"Couldn't the strange priests and their god have taken Hakon and Rark prisoners, or changed them by witchcraft into the gulls that I saw flying in the air?" I wondered to myself anxiously.

"Thor, may your hammer strike Hakon's enemies!" I said aloud. It occurred to me then that I was in Frankland, and here the god of the new religion reigned. "God of the Franks," I added, "let not your priests do evil to Hakon."

I do not know how long I stood there looking out towards the Island of Saint Michel. I was thinking about the gods. I had begun to explain to myself why the gods that rule in the north had to be different from those whom men believe in in the south, when I remembered that Thora Magnusdaughter and many others in Tronhjem had believed in the new god before Earl Hakon had forbidden his worship.

Suddenly I saw Hakon, Rark and the other men pushing their boat down to the water. One of the men was carrying great bundles, which he put very carefully into the stern.

"Bread!" I exclaimed. The thought of eating fresh bread again made me happy.

I could see that they were having a difficult time pushing the boat into the water, but I did not wait to watch them row back. I ran to the beach, in the hope that I should be the first to carry the good news of their return.

The bread of the Franks must be the kind of bread that men eat in Odin's hall, for it is light and made from a grain that does not grow in Norway. Also in greens, the Franks are rich; while we in the north know only cabbage and onions, they have many strange and wonderful-tasting vegetables.

Hakon had brought with him a small barrel of wine. There was only one cupful for each of us. It tasted not at all like mead. It was a little sour. We were all disappointed, and some of the men swore that it tasted worse than the watered mead that is given to children at feasts.

We had decided to stay the night on the island and sail the following morning at high tide. That evening, when I saw Hakon walking alone on the beach, I approached him. I wanted to hear about the strange priests who lived on the Island of Saint Michel.

"The high priest has four heads: one pointed in each direction that the winds come from. He sat mounted on a dragon . . . I think it was the Midgard Worm."

Thinking his words were true, I asked breathlessly, "Weren't you frightened?"

"Terribly," Hakon answered. "The dragon spoke Norse, and I talked with him while Rark talked to the priest."

While Hakon spoke, I tried to look at him, but he kept turning his head away. Still, I caught a glimpse of his smile, and I realized what a fool I had been. This made me angry, and I was determined not to speak again until Hakon said he was sorry.

"The high priest was very old, and wore a cloak of the same material as Hjalte Gudbrandson's."

I walked on as if Hakon were not speaking.

"I think they were frightened of us, for they gave me all the things that I wanted to buy."

Hakon caught up with me, and touching my chin turned my face towards his. His expression was so serious that I began to laugh. My laughter made me forget the four-headed priest and the Midgard Worm. Soon I was asking questions and listening eagerly to Hakon's answers.

The most important news they had received from the priests was that Rark's uncle was the high priest of the Church of Saint Malo; and certainly, he could be of help to Rark.

"Why have they built a temple on that small island, it is so barren?" I asked and pointed towards the Island of Saint Michel, where the setting sun was reflecting itself in the windows of the church.

"I don't know. The high priest said they will make it even larger soon; and one day, the temple will cover the whole island."

I glanced at the mainland with its marshes. "Yes, the island is well protected," I said thoughtfully. "What is that which shines?" Now Hakon explained to me what glass could do: let in the sun, but keep out the wind. "Saint Malo, what strange names they have here in Frankland."

"Saint means 'sacred to the new god.' " Hakon said.

"Are there more people in Saint Malo than there are on the Island of Saint Michel?"

"It is bigger than Tronhjem, and Rark's uncle is the ruler of it all."

I thought of Rark; and all that he had told me— when we were slaves — about his life as a freeman in Frankland. Suddenly I realized that I had never really believed him. I had thought his stories were dreams like my own, of having a father who was king. Now I knew why he had not behaved like a slave: the land he had visited at night, when he closed his eyes, he had once known in the noon light, when all dreams vanish.

"Our luck holds like the hair that binds the Fenris Wolf," Hakon said.

I feared that to mention our good fortune too often was to tempt the gods, so I asked Hakon quickly, "Were there only men on the Island of Saint Michel?"

"Oh no! The high priest has a wife as pretty as the setting sun, and seven daughters, each as beautiful as the moon."

I took a handful of sand and threw it at Hakon, for even I knew that the priests of the new god did not marry. Hakon reached out for me. I tossed another handful of sand at him; this time some of it went into his eyes. I ran quickly towards the center of the island. When I reached the rock that at high tide was half covered by the sea, I turned around. Hakon had not run after me. I was afraid that he was angry, but my pride told me to walk on.

At the end of the boulders that fringe the beach, I saw Magnus the Fair coming towards me. I called his name but he did not answer. His face was flushed and he turned in another direction.

Soon I came to a meadow, which was covered with a kind of grass whose blades are so tough that they can cut the skin like little knives. In the midst of it sat Rigmor Ragnvaldsdaughter, her face disfigured by tears. I stood perfectly still, not knowing what to do. Finally, I

took a step forward and softly called her name.

Rigmor got up and looked at me with such hatred that I dared not go near her; then she grabbed a stone that lay at her feet and threw it at me.

The stone missed. It passed above my shoulder, near my left ear, and fell with a clatter behind me. Too surprised to move, I repeated her name. Rigmor turned and ran. I looked behind me, to see if I could find the stone Rigmor had thrown. But there were many stones and they all looked alike.

21

H AKON'S LUCK was with us when we came to Saint
Malo, as it had been with us in Tronhjem and when we
met King Olaf Trygveson's ships. But summer does not
stay, fall will come; and surely luck cannot last forever. What had been told on the Island of Saint Michel
was true: Rark's uncle was, indeed, high priest of the
church at Saint Malo. He was a tall, old man. He
treated us with much kindness and even helped Hakon
to sell his skins and buy wares that we either needed on
Rogen, or we knew would fetch good prices in Tronhjem.

The town was built on a rocky island, which at low
tide was connected with the mainland. Almost all the
houses were small. They were built of stone and had
thatch roofs. Most of the men were fishermen, but
some worked building a new church. It was to be a
great stone temple. Rark's uncle had many plans. He
also wanted to build a wall around the whole town to
protect it from strangers. I guessed that if he had had a
wall around his town, he might not have been so kind
to us.

Our camp was not in the town of Saint Malo, but on

a small island to the south. It was at the entrance of the fjord, which, from Saint Malo, flows far inland. The lonely life on Rogen had taught us not to make enemies needlessly; and the people of Saint Malo left us in peace, for they were much frightened of Norsemen.

The land around Saint Malo was poor. Though the Norsemen held all of Normandy, none of them had settled here; but the names of the great Norse chieftains and warriors were well known among the men of Saint Malo. Rark made a point of telling everyone that Hakon was a near kin of Duke Richard the Second of Normandy. Hakon did not like this, for it was a lie. But Rark pointed out to him that we were so few that we needed the protection of the Duke's name.

"Besides," he said, "are not all Norsemen kin?"

When I heard Rark say this, I was reminded that he was not a Norseman. All the men now treated Rark differently: with more respect and a little awe; as one might a stranger whom one trusted, but whom one could never really understand.

From his uncle, Rark learned that his wife and children were alive. Rark wanted to set out immediately for his hall; but the priest said it would be wiser to send someone ahead of him, to announce his coming. Rark was perplexed by this suggestion: why should not he, himself, be the messenger of his own good tidings? But the priest insisted, he spoke of unexpected dangers; and finally, he told Rark that since he had lived for many years among unbelievers, he would have to cleanse himself. Rark agreed to wait fifteen days, and a man whom the priest knew was sent to Rark's hall.

Rark no longer lived at our camp, for the priest had demanded that he live at his house and attend the daily offering to the new god, which is called Mass.

While Rark lived with his uncle, we made ourselves as comfortable as we could. We built an oven for the baking of bread, and tasted cow's meat again. On the morning of the fifteenth day, Rark returned to our camp to talk with Erp the Traveler and Hakon the Lucky. From his face, one could judge that the news he brought was not pleasant. When he had finished talking with Erp and Hakon, their faces were grim, as well.

The messenger had not yet returned; but that morning, Rark's uncle had told him why he had opposed his returning to his hall at once. Two years ago Rark's wife had married again. Her husband was a Frank, named Hugues, who was the half brother of the Count of Paris. Rark's uncle had sent a message to Hugues, reminding him that according to the laws of Frankland, and those of the new god, Hugues would have to leave his wife and give up her property, for the woman he had married had not been a widow and had had no right to marry again.

When Rark had finished his story, Erp had said angrily, "Only a fool would wake a bear before he takes aim at it!"

Rark, too, was angry at his uncle for having deceived him, and for having given warning to his enemy. Only Hakon, who recounted the conversation to the rest of us, seemed to understand the priest's behavior.

The following day Rark and Hakon went to Saint Malo, to speak with Rark's uncle and to buy horses.

156

After much talking, an agreement was made with the priest that for a certain amount of gold, he would supply the part of the crew that remained behind with *Munin* with all their needs, and would use his influence to protect both ship and men. He insisted that Rark wait two more days in Saint Malo, until the messenger returned. When Erp heard this he said, "The priest will speak with that messenger no more while he walks this earth." But Erp had only patience to wait for the winds, not for men.

Hakon had only been able to buy five horses, and they were not young. Magnus the Fair said of them that he dared not look at their teeth, for fear they didn't have any.

Hakon announced that Hakon the Black; his wife, Gretha; Astrid Erpsdaughter; and four of the older men should remain behind to guard *Munin*. I was sorry that Rigmor Ragnvaldsdaughter was not to stay on the island south of Saint Malo; but I dared say nothing of it to Hakon, for fear that he would order me to stay behind.

On the day of our departure, Rark and Hakon went again to visit the priest, for he had sent two men to our camp to say that he had news of great importance. Erp the Traveler claimed that this was merely a new way of detaining us; but when Rark and Hakon, who liked and trusted the priest, returned, we found out that Erp had been wrong.

The messenger whom Rark's uncle had sent to Rark's hall had at last returned. Hugues had kept him prisoner for several days while he — Hugues — had traveled to another priest, one who was called a bishop and was much more important than Rark's uncle. This bishop had declared that Rark had stayed so long away from his home, and dwelt so long among barbarians, that his wife had been within her rights to marry again, and that Hugues was her only husband.

Rark had become furious when he heard this. His uncle had then said to him that there were higher priests than this bishop. "I could travel to see the Pope, while Hugues laughs as he sits at my table!" Rark had cried. (The Pope is the highest priest of all the Christians, and lives in a country far, far to the south.)

In his fury, Rark had accused his uncle of being in the pay of Hugues. At this the old priest also had grown angry. "Many years you have been away, and God has tried you much. Sad has been your fate. But at the point of a sword, one does not win back a wife. I have been godfather to your son, and for his sake I beg you, keep your temper in your heart, and your sword in your scabbard."

Rark and his uncle parted as friends; and the priest promised to pray to the new god that Rark's journey would end well; that he would receive what was justly his, without bloodshed.

It was late afternoon when we had tied the bundles onto the horses and were ready to start. We marched south along the shore of the fjord. When the sun was about to set, we passed a ridge. Without a word or a sign from anyone, we all looked back at the island on which *Munin* was beached, and at the town of Saint Malo.

"Before the sun has set fifteen times, we shall return!" shouted Thorkild Erikson.

Orm, who stood near me, said, "By the gods, and Hakon's luck, we shall return to Rogen so rich that we shall drink from silver cups!"

22

TWENTY-FOUR MEN and three women, even though
they are well armed, do not make an army. True, in the
old tales no hero needed more than his sword to slay
the giants. But the songs of old are told at night, when
dreams are near and the flickering light of the fire has
painted the walls.

On the first part of our expedition the summer sun
shone, and left but few shadows for the poet to sing of.
We walked along the fjord. The first night we did not
camp. At the end of the fjord, the land rises to a
great plateau, and at the edge of this plateau lies Dinan.
We came to Dinan by the afternoon of the second day.
When we saw it, our courage left us: it was a town
much larger than Saint Malo. We dared not go near it.
Rark, who had family in the town, set out alone, on
foot, to visit them.

We made camp near the shore, feeling — though we
were boatless — that the sea was our friend and somehow we were not alone when we were near it. After
we had eaten the evening meal, sentries were posted
and half of us were free to sleep.

I could not sleep. I walked south along the coast, until I came to our sentry. It was Magnus the Fair. He was sitting leaning against the trunk of a tree, looking up towards the town of Dinan. His bow and arrows rested on the ground beside him. He did not turn at my approach, and I thought he had not heard me, until he suddenly spoke: "Soft are the sparrow's steps."

I smiled and sat down beside him. "And meaningless its song."

"No," Magnus said, "not meaningless: it is the song of the earth, the song of the seed breaking through the frost-hard ground, saying to the world, 'I want to live!'"

"And what about the eagle's song?" I asked and looked over the water, towards the other shore of the fjord.

"An eagle screams, it does not sing."

I turned and looked at Magnus. "What is it, it screams?"

Magnus looked away, as if he did not want me to see his face. "The world is mine, fear me!" He touched his beard with his hand; and then he continued to speak, but as if he were talking to himself, or to a stranger whom he knew well, yet I had never met. "It circles in the air, so far away from the earth that it no longer belongs to it. And if another eagle comes near it, it attacks, as if the whole sky were not large enough for two eagles. Men say, 'free as an eagle,' but that bird has made of the wide sky a cage even smaller than the kind we make of willow branches."

I felt, then, what many men spoke of feeling when

they listened to Magnus: I was frightened and cold. "But the sparrows admire the eagle," I mumbled, and bit at the nail of my thumb.

"True, and that is why I pity them." Magnus paused, but I said nothing, for I felt he had not finished speaking. "And that is why I hate them, too!"

Magnus the Fair jumped up and took his bow from the ground. He stood still for a moment, contemplating it as if he had never seen it before; then he looked down at me: "But, Helga, what are you?"

I smiled up at him and said, "A duck, I think sometimes." Then I laughed. "Quack . . . quack . . ."

Magnus laughed, too, and flung himself down beside me. "Those words in duck language mean: 'I am very contented with myself.'"

It pleased me so much to see Magnus laugh that I did not mind his making fun of me. I pointed towards Dinan, above us. "As big a town as that, I do not think there is in all of Norway."

Magnus looked up at the town; torches were burning on the low ramparts that surrounded it. "No, I do not think it is an eagle's nest . . . What worries me more is, what kind of man is Hugues?"

I had given little thought to Hugues. "He is a brute, or he would have followed the orders of the priest and left a wife that was not his!"

Magnus grinned. "'Quack . . . quack . . .' said the duck, 'the sea was made for the duck to swim in, and the sun for drying its feathers.'"

Magnus' remark hurt me and I grew silent.

"You like Rark because he has been kind to you.

Hugues, you do not know; therefore Rark must be right and Hugues wrong."

There was never any pleasure in admitting to Magnus that you were wrong, so I said nothing, though within myself I knew that what he had said was true.

"Rark has been away for many winters, all who knew him thought him dead. A dead man does not enter unpunished the world of the living."

"But she is his wife!" I said.

Magnus shook his head. "No, she is not. Do you know that Rark has another name among the Franks? He is called Jacques de Bardinais."

I tried to say the strange name, but my tongue got in the way of the words. "I think I like Rark better."

"But his wife would not. Her husband was Jacques de Bardinais, not Rark of Rogen."

Magnus' words had given me much to think about, for it was true that Jacques de "something I could not pronounce" was as foreign to me as Hugues; perhaps even more so, for at least Hugues' name I could say. I wanted to be alone to think the matter over. I got up. "But Hugues is a brute, I am sure he is," I said.

As I turned in the direction of the camp, I thought that I heard Magnus utter a low "quack" as a parting word; but when I looked back at him, he said thoughtfully, "Of that I have no doubt either, for most men are brutes." A moment later he called after me, "And most women, too!" I could think of no sharp word to match his, so I let silence be my reply.

The place that Magnus had chosen for his post was the center of a small field, where a little group of trees and boulders gave him shelter, should he be attacked. A low ridge of stones and bushes lay between the meadow and our camp. When I came near it, a bush moved. Rigmor Ragnvaldsdaughter was crouching behind it. I had seen her move. From her hiding place, she must have been watching Magnus and me.

I decided as I walked towards her that it was wiser to act as if I had not seen her. I changed my direction a little, so that I would pass the ridge farther away from her hiding place.

When I reached the center of the ridge, I heard her call my name. I stopped; but then I decided that it was better to walk on. I heard her running after me; and finally, I turned around.

Rigmor's face was white as new-fallen snow except for two red blotches on her cheeks. "Are you afraid, slave?" she cried.

I looked at her belt to see if she had a weapon, but she had none.

"Why do you play with him?"

I was shocked and I answered stupidly, "Who?"

Rigmor believed that I had intended to insult her; of this I am sure, for she could not understand my childishness.

"You don't want him!" she shouted.

I nodded; for truly, in the sense that a woman wants to love a man, I did not want Magnus the Fair.

"I hate you!"

This I knew so well that it surprised me that she would say it; and even more, that I should be frightened on hearing it. "But Magnus does not love you!"

The words had escaped me, though they were foolish and I could have bitten my tongue for saying them.

"He shall love no one but me."

I shook my head, half in wonder and half in pity; but Rigmor was so filled with anger that she could not understand anything but what was burning inside herself. She started to laugh hysterically. Suddenly she screamed at me, "You have bewitched him! You have cast a spell on him! Here, slave, take my arm ring and give him back to me!" Then she took the arm ring and held it out towards me.

"I know nothing of spells," I whispered.

Rigmor threw the arm ring at my feet. Glaring at me, she cried, "Pick it up! Pick it up!"

"Don't," said a voice from behind.

I turned and saw Magnus the Fair standing but a few steps away from me. His face was as pale as Rigmor's, and his eyes seemed gray with anger.

I felt tears coming into my eyes, and I turned from both of them. I ran towards the camp. It was dusk, I did not watch where I was running, and I fell. One of my knees hurt; but I got up as quickly as I could, for I feared hearing what Magnus would say to Rigmor Ragnvaldsdaughter.

When I came near the camp, I stopped and sat down upon the ground. I cried silently and rubbed my sore knee. Over and over again, I said to myself, "I wish that I were back on Rogen, and that I were a child again!"

23

WE PASSED the town of Dinan and pushed on south. But the memory of the size of that town, and the fact that we no longer had the sea to look upon, made us uneasy. Even the young men did not laugh as readily as they had before. In this part of Frankland, the country is covered by forests; we hunted and ate well, for there were many deer. When we came to a clearing, where people lived and the fields were plowed, we walked closer together, and each kept an arrow on his bow-string.

The second night after we left Dinan, we stayed at a farm that belonged to a friend of Rark's. This farm looked like most of the other farms we had seen. There were four or five stone houses with thatched roofs, all of them very small except the house of the owner. In the main house, there was a fireplace with a chimney for letting out the smoke. This seemed to me much better than our open fire, which so often is smoky and causes tears to come into one's eyes. But the houses in Frankland must be very damp in winter, for even now, in summer, the walls were very wet. In Norway, we use stone only for the storehouses and the sheds for the animals; the halls are built of wood.

Rark's friends were not unkind to us; yet we felt that they were happier to see us leave than they had been at our arrival. Our plan was to march to the church called Saint Meen, which was not far from Rark's hall. From there we would send a message to Hugues. Hakon thought that with gold, one might persuade Hugues to give up what was not his own.

The last night before we came to Saint Meen, we camped in a clearing in the woods. After our evening meal, Rark told us of the great magician, Merlin, who had once lived in a stone tower in these woods. He had loved a fairy, named Vivienne; and she — because she loved him, too — had drawn a magic circle around the tower, so that Merlin could never leave her.

Hakon, who was sitting beside me, was fond of this kind of story. I watched his face while Rark told of an ancient king, who had been Merlin's friend. I do not like stories about magicians, elves, or trolls, as much as Hakon does; for my mind always stops at one place in the story, and starts to go its own way. So it was this evening. While Rark's story went on, my thoughts stayed with Vivienne: had she really loved the magician? Why did she need a magic circle to bind him to her? If she truly loved him, would she not have taken away the spell?

I looked towards the fire. On the other side of it sat Rigmor Ragnvaldsdaughter. "No," I thought, "if the fairy had been Rigmor, she never would have let the magician leave the tower." From Rigmor, my thoughts passed to Hakon's father and Thora Magnusdaughter. I closed my eyes and tried to see their faces. Thora would never have tried to hold Olaf Sigurdson with anything less than her love.

"Oh, to have lived in those times!"

Startled, I realized that Rark had finished his story, and Hakon was talking to me. I nodded, though I did not know if I wanted to live in a time when there were so many trolls and magicians.

"Why do we all like to dream of times that are past?" I looked with surprise at the speaker. It was Ketil Ragnvaldson, who usually was too shy to talk when more than four ears could hear him.

"Because we have all once been children."

I knew the speaker was Magnus the Fair, and I did not look up. Since my last meeting with Rigmor, I had tried to keep away from Magnus, and had done my best not to notice him.

"What do you mean, Magnus?"

Hakon's question made me smile to myself, for though I could not have explained Magnus the Fair's words, I felt I knew what he meant. Magnus started to say something, but he was interrupted by one of the sentries, who called out from his post.

We all grabbed our bows. Luckily it was not an attack, for it was a poor place we had chosen to camp. The clearing was just small enough so that arrows could be shot at us from the safety of the forest.

The sentry, Nils Haroldson, had captured an old man. He looked like a slave: barefooted and ill-clad. He spoke the Franks' language and did not understand what Nils had been asking him.

When Rark spoke to him in his own language, the

old man suddenly threw himself on his knees and kissed Rark's hand. Had he been silent before, he now spoke so much that one tongue did not seem to be enough for him. Several times Rark stopped him to ask questions; then the man nodded and shook his head, as if the enforced silence were too much for him, and not being able to speak with his mouth, he needed to talk with his head.

When finally Rark had finished speaking with him, the Frank was given food and drink. While he ate, we crowded around Rark to hear what he had said.

Although Rark did not recognize him, the old man said that he had been a servant of Rark's father, and claimed to be loyal to Rark as well. I did not believe him, for he had the manners of a slave. A slave's real masters are his fear and his hunger; therefore, he cannot be trusted.

At first Rark had hoped that the servant had been sent by his wife; but the servant had explained that Maria (for that was Rark's wife's name) was loyal to Hugues because he had bewitched her by giving her a love potion to drink. The old man said that Hugues could not be bought with gold, nor would he listen to the words of priests; Rark's only hope lay in attacking the hall, which was almost defenseless. But we must attack at once and not stop at the Church of Saint Meen, for Hugues had sent messengers to the hall of his half brother for help. Twelve of Hugues' own men were serving his half brother, and these — if not many more — would be certain to arrive in a few days.

When Rark had finished speaking, his face had the

same bitter sadness I had seen so often on Hakon's father's face.

"Many a man kisses the hand of him he plans to destroy," said Erp the Traveler. "I have been in the south before. Here men like plots as much as our women do in the north."

"Let us show that we are Norsemen!" Eigil Haroldson shouted. "Let us attack at once!"

Several of the younger men agreed with Eigil. Hakon and Rark said nothing, for they knew the decision was theirs.

For the first time, I spoke at council. I was trembling, and I could not form my thoughts into poetry, as I knew one should at moments of great importance.

"I am Helga Gunhildsdaughter. I was born the slave of Olaf Sigurdson and he treated me kindly; but when he died I became the slave of Sigurd Sigurdson, the traitor, who gave me to Eirik the Fox, a cruel and cunning master. When Hakon Olafson was hiding for his life in the cave in the Mountain of the Sun, I was sent to climb that mountain, for Sigurd and Eirik hoped that Hakon would see me and come out of his hiding place, to meet his death. The message of a slave is worded by his master."

Magnus the Fair jumped to his feet. "Have I not told you, Hakon the Lucky, that Helga is a Valkyrie sent by the gods to protect us!"

I walked away from the fire; having spoken made me feel so strange that I could not stay. When I returned, it had been decided that we should rest for the night.

Of all that had been said, the old Frank servant was only told that we would wait until morning before planning our course. Now he begged Rark to be allowed to go back to the hall at once, saying that he would open the big doors of the halls for us, so that we would not need to scale the walls. Rark told him that he must wait until morning. The old man's last suggestion made me more sure than ever that he was a spy for Hugues.

Since the clearing was small and tomorrow might be a day of battle, Hakon ordered only one man, Orm the Storyteller, to stand guard; but we were all to sleep with our bows and arrows next to us.

Sleep is a difficult guest to keep out, when once he has knocked at your door; but I was determined to keep awake in order to watch the old man. Not far from me, he was lying on his stomach, his face resting between his hands, so that no one could see his eyes. Orm the Storyteller was sitting by the fire, but I did not dare turn my head to see if he had fallen asleep; tired as I was, myself, from the day's march, I could not have blamed him if he had. Around me I heard the sounds of the sleeping men, and my will to stay awake was steadily weakening.

I was dozing when I heard someone move. I opened my eyes. The Frank had lifted his head and was looking around. I closed my eyes again, and pressed the lids together so hard that I saw fire. When I opened them, the old man was crawling on all fours towards the forest. "Through the forest, he knows his way," I thought, "and we shall never recapture him."

I fitted an arrow on the bowstring. As the Frank rose

171

from a crouching position and started to run, I shot. The arrow hit him in the back. He sank to his knees; then he tried to rise again, but he fell, face down upon the ground. I did not hear him cry out; but he must have, for suddenly, everyone was awake.

I walked slowly towards the body of the old man, knowing all the time that I had killed him. A group of men were standing around him when I came. Among them were Hakon and Rark. Hakon looked at me strangely, as if he were seeing me for the first time. I looked into his eyes. I wanted to say, "Yes, it is I!" Instead I mumbled, "He was trying to escape."

Rark knelt down and closed the old man's eyes; then he made over him the Christian's sign, with his fingers. I wanted desperately to speak with Rark; but I did not know what I wanted to say, and when he stood up, I found I could only turn away.

Now I knew why we loved the tales of old, for through them we can live unpunished. Siegfried's death does not move us, for had Guttorm's sword not pierced him, the rusty sword of age would long ago have felled him. But that old man, that servant, that slave, that Frank: his sun set because of one of my arrows. Real death is silent and we cannot describe it.

I walked alone when we marched towards Saint Meen. When Hakon, seeing me crying, came up to me, I turned away. I knew that from that day onward, part of me would always walk alone.

24

THE CHURCH OF SAINT MEEN was larger than the one in Saint Malo, but no town surrounded it. There were only a few buildings, all close to the church: three that housed the priests and their servants, and two stables for their animals. In Saint Meen lived many priests: thirteen or fourteen, at least; perhaps there were more, for it was hard to tell the difference between the poorer priests and the servants. I believe that priests and servants, together, numbered as many people as we were; but that, too, I cannot say with certainty, for we were not allowed to make our camp near the buildings.

When we arrived early in the morning, walking close together with our bows in our hands, we were met an arrow's shot from the church by the high priest. He was followed by ten other priests. One of them, a very young man, was carrying a picture of the new god on a pole in front of him. Rark spoke to them, and asked if we might make a camp near the buildings.

The high priest replied by asking if we were Christians. Rark answered that he was and the priest bid him kneel and kiss the picture of the god. Rark kneeled down, and the picture which was painted on a piece of scarlet cloth was lowered so that Rark could kiss the hem of it. When the priest demanded that the rest of us do the same, Rark had to admit that we were not Christians. On hearing this, the high priest said that we could not stay near the church, but he offered us a small shed in the middle of a nearby field, and said we might use that.

The men grumbled and said that the priest had insulted their honor; but Magnus the Fair said, "Honor is too dear a cloak for a beggar to wear."

This truth was a bitter drink for us to swallow, but several of the men walked silently in the direction of the hut. Hakon ordered the rest to follow, and to take the horses with them. This they did, though Eigil Haroldson found it necessary for his pride to spit on the ground before he walked away.

Rark continued speaking with the priest, and Hakon stayed at his side. Just as Freya the Young and I were about to follow the men, the young priest who had carried the banner with the god's picture on it approached us, and to our amazement, spoke to us in the Norse language.

He told us that his parents had come from Norway, near More, and that he had been given the name of Guttorm when he was born.

"Is that not your name now?" asked Freya the Young. "Surely, the name given to you by your parents you cannot throw away like a broken pot."

The priest explained that his parents had been killed when he was twelve winters old, and he had been brought up by the priests who had given him the name of Michel. He also told us that it was common among

Norsemen, when they changed their gods, to change their names as well.

I thought long about this and found much sense in it; for a change of name might fool the old gods, so they would not know who you were, and there would be less chance of their taking revenge upon you. I would not have minded changing my name, for I had never liked the name of Helga. I stopped listening to what the priest was saying. I was thinking about what name I should choose. I decided upon Thora, the name that Hakon's stepmother had. "Thora Gunhildsdaughter," I said to myself, and smiled for the sound of the name pleased me.

"Helga." I looked up confused, for in my mind I was already Thora. It was Hakon calling to us, from a distance.

The young priest turned and said farewell. When Hakon joined us, we told him about how one could change one's name when one believed in the new god. Hakon walked beside us silently, and we knew that he was troubled. Rark had remained behind to attend Mass at the church. "What did the high priest tell Rark?" I asked.

Hakon looked back towards the church, which was the most beautiful building of its kind we had yet seen. "The new god is a god of peace, but there was no peace in the eyes of this priest, whom they call Father Christopher."

I asked Hakon if Rark had not known the high priest when he had been master of his own hall.

"No," Hakon replied. "Father Christopher has been here but a few winters. The old priest who was Rark's friend is dead, as are all the other priests that Rark knew who lived in Saint Meen."

I looked up at Hakon with surprise for certainly it was strange that all the priests had died. "Norsemen," he began bitterly, "raided the Church of Saint Meen four winters ago and killed all the priests . . . Since we arrived in Saint Malo, we have had little luck. I fear our gods are not strong in Frankland."

I caught hold of Hakon's sleeve and was trying to think of something to say when Freya the Young exclaimed, "Hakon the Lucky, let us pray to the new god. If this is his country, why not please him?"

Hakon smiled. He looked first at the ground, and then up at the sky. "If only Balder's time would come. When he walks the earth, then all men will be friends and swords rust."

"Could not the new god be Balder?" I asked uncertainly.

Hakon shook his head. "Remember, Helga . . . Remember King Olaf Trygveson's ships! That King has claimed he will make all of Norway believe in the new god. I saw the sun shine on the shields and swords of his hird. The only message he brought me was an arrow. King Olaf has not changed his gods, only their names."

"But the priest in Saint Malo," I argued.

Hakon nodded. "Yes, he was a good man. There were no clouds of evil in his eyes, only the sadness of knowledge. But my father was a good man, too, and so was Earl Hakon's father, Earl Sigurd; and they both believed in Odin."

We were almost at the shed. Freya the Young had gone on ahead of us. "Hakon," I said softly, "do not tell the men that you fear you left your luck behind you; for when men doubt their luck, their arms grow weak."

Hakon smiled and put his arm about my shoulders.

We made of our sheepcot as good a storehouse as we could, keeping all of our supplies inside it. The night was warm; and none of us had any wish to sleep within the low walls of the shed, which smelled so strongly.

Though we had not loaded the horses heavily, two of them could not carry their share. One of these we slaughtered. The Franks, like all Christians, seldom eat horsemeat; and the two servants of the priests, who carried out the barrels of wine Hakon had bought, regarded our meal with disgust.

The moon was nearly full. When it rose, Hakon and Rark decided to set out for Rark's hall to spy on it. They took three men with them, among them Magnus the Fair. I walked with them as far as the forest. Hakon promised that they would be back before the moon set, for Rark's hall was not far away.

I was walking back to the camp to join those sitting around the fire when I noticed that Rigmor Ragnvalds-daughter was among them. Changing the direction of my steps, I walked towards the church. A dim light was shining through one of its windows. When I was an arrow's shot away from it, I halted and sat down upon the ground. An owl flew by me, with its silent wings. I watched it land on top of the roof of the church and then fly away again. "It probably spied a mouse for its supper," I thought.

The walls of the church were almost white in the moonlight; but at the corners lurked darkness. A shadow came out of the night, looked around, and then walked rapidly towards me.

The black robes of the priest made him appear unreal, until he was quite near and I could see his face. It was the young Norseman whom we had spoken to that morning. "Michel," I called softly.

He stopped, looked around; then came over to me. "I have come to speak with your chieftain," he said, keeping his voice very low.

"He has gone," I answered. I did not get up, but asked him to sit down, as if the field were my hall and he my guest. He sat down carefully, and I guessed that he was not used to making a bench of the earth.

"What have you to tell him?"

At my question, the priest looked back at the church he had come from, as if he were afraid that the building could be listening. "I have come to warn him," he whispered.

"You are the second person who has come to warn us. At our last camp a Frank servant came to tell us not to come to Saint Meen, but to attack Hugues at once."

"I see you did not listen to him. He was an old man, poorly dressed, wasn't he?"

"How do you know?"

"I saw him ride by here yesterday morning with Hugues. It is well that you did not listen to the old man, he was a spy."

I was relieved to hear this; yet I turned away from the priest. "We killed him!" I blurted out.

The young priest made the Christian's sign; but I did not give him a chance to speak. "We have sailed a long way, and left our homes, to bring our friend back to Frankland and his wife . . . Rark is a Christian like you or the man you call Father Christopher, yet you will not help us!"

The young priest bowed his head. "Father Christopher comes from a great Frank family. One of his brothers was a priest here at Saint Meen when the Norsemen, who killed all the priests, came."

"But Rark is not a Norseman," I argued.

"Hugues has given silver candlesticks to our church, and is the protector of our abbey."

I wondered what an abbey was, but I was too concerned with presenting Rark's cause to ask. "Rark would protect you as well, once he sits in the high seat, in his own hall!"

The priest looked again up at the large building, with the cross on its gable. "Many heavy duties has our god placed on our shoulders, but none is harder than the one that we must love our enemies, and when they strike us, that we should not strike back."

I nodded, for I was thinking of Rigmor. "Your parents were killed by the Franks, weren't they?"

For the first time, the priest looked at me when he

answered. "My father had been very cruel to those who killed him. It was a sin to have killed him. But I forgive those who did it, for he had left them without hope."

"I have been without hope once," I said, and I wondered if his father had been like Hakon's uncle, Sigurd Sigurdson, or Eirik the Fox. For a long time, we both were silent; then I asked, "Where are Rark's children?"

"Hugues has sent Jacques de Bardinais' children, and all the servants who might be faithful to him, to another hall, far to the south of here," he explained in a whisper.

"What is it you have come to warn us about?"

Quickly the priest glanced over his shoulder. "Hugues has gathered in his hall five times the number of men that follow your chieftain."

"Five times!" I rose from the ground. "Five times!" I repeated.

The priest did not stir until I spoke thanking him; then he leapt to his feet as if he had been sitting on a glowing ember.

"I shall tell our leader what you have told me," I said. "It is very kind of you to warn us."

The priest smiled, nodded, and turned to walk away; but he took only a few steps before he halted and looked back at me. "I shall pray for you."

I thought I saw the smile fade from his face, and his eyes grow sad. I watched him walk towards the church, until he melted into the night.

I walked back to the camp. Everyone, except the

guards, was asleep. I sat down near the dying fire, waiting my turn to stand guard. Staring at the embers, I thought, "So the Frank I killed was a spy!" Yet I did not close my eyes, for fear of seeing his dead face.

25

THE SKY WAS BLOOD-RED in the east when Hakon, Rark, Magnus the Fair, Ketil Ragnvaldson, and Nils Harold-son returned. They looked very tired. Quickly I told them of my conversation with the priest. When I finished, Rark sighed.

"I came here to find my life; and all that Saint Meen seems to have to offer me is a grave . . . And for my friends, the same." Rark looked towards the forest, in the direction of his home. "I have visited myself to-night. Jacques de Bardinais died long ago. I did not know, for I was not invited to the burial. Only Rark, the slave of the barbarians, lives."

"You are not a slave!" Hakon said. I could see that Rark's words had hurt Hakon, for he was used to re-garding Rark almost as if he were his father.

Rark put his hand on Hakon's shoulder. "It is hard to lose twice that which you love; and bitter to find the door of your own house locked against you."

Hakon's face grew red with embarrassment and he spoke haltingly. "No man is homeless who has a friend's hall to live in."

Again Rark sighed. "Ungratefulness can make a beg-gar of a king. We are alive still. Sharp are our swords;

and even Job must have laughed, when he got tired of tears."

I wanted to ask whether Job was a Frank hero; but Rark looked so sad I dared not speak to him.

When we sat down to our morning meal, we felt more cheerful and thought that five Franks to one Norseman was, after all, not such terrible odds. Hakon had arranged, through Rark, that the priests at Saint Meen should supply us with bread, milk, and cheese. The milk was creamy, and Magnus the Fair declared that it would be well if all those who kept cows in Norway believed in the new god, since he forbids the watering of milk. At this, even Rark laughed.

"Many a man in Frankland thinks it is easier to milk a stream than a cow," Rark said.

When we had finished eating, a servant of the priests came to ask Rark and Hakon to accompany them to the church, for Father Christopher wanted to talk with them. Hakon shrugged his shoulders, as if he thought more talk would not help Rark's cause, but he rose; and he and Rark walked off in the direction of the buildings.

They were not gone long; and they were grave and troubled when they returned. The men crowded around them, and Hakon said, as he smiled a crooked smile, "We have been invited to a feast."

"To a feast?" Erp asked unbelievingly.

"At Rark's hall. Hugues has invited us," Hakon explained.

"Don't go!" I said. "Don't go!"

Rark said nothing. Finally, Hakon told us that Hugues had sent a message to the high priest, saying that he was willing to discuss Rark's grievances with him. Hugues had invited Rark, Hakon, and three men, whom Rark was to choose from Hakon's hird, to come to the hall. Father Christopher and four of his priests were to be present at the meeting, as guarantee for the Norsemen's safety.

"And what did you say?" Erp asked.

"We said we would come," Hakon answered.

"Then I shall come, too!" I shouted. When Hakon did not reply, I said, "If you do not take me, then I shall follow you anyway."

Rark looked at me thoughtfully, then he said, "Let her come. I trust Father Christopher's word. We shall be safe enough."

It was decided that Erp the Traveler, Nils Haroldson, and myself should accompany Rark and Hakon to Hugues' feast. Magnus the Fair was to be in charge of the men at Saint Meen. If we should not return by nightfall, he would lead the men towards Rark's hall.

The five of us who were to be Hugues' guests walked down to the small stream and washed ourselves. The men had their beards trimmed and I brushed my hair. When we had finished, Magnus the Fair looked at us and then, laughing, he said, "Judge not a Norseman by his clothes, or you will mistake him for a beggar."

"True," I answered, "our appearance will not blind Hugues like the sun, his eyes shall not compare us to eagles, but neither shall his nose be reminded of hogs when we sit at table with him."

Magnus took a silver arm ring, made in the shape of a snake, and put it on my arm. "Let them not think us so poor that we allow only the gods to adorn our women."

I looked at the arm ring. It was very beautiful. Magnus had bought it in Saint Malo, and had used nearly all the silver that he owned to pay for it. "I shall take good care of it, and bring it back to you."

Magnus stared long at me; then he wrinkled his nose. "Bring back both the ring and the arm, for I wish to own both of them."

I looked away, for no words came to me that would not hurt him. Then I saw Hakon approaching us, and I was grateful that I would not have to answer Magnus.

Hakon's face was stern as he gave his final orders to Magnus the Fair. "If we should be slain by Hugues, do not try to avenge us, but take the men and lead them back to *Munin* and to Rogen. What is on board *Munin* you can sell in Tronhjem. The profit should be shared in such a way that none among the crew need complain of having been unjustly treated. A third of the profit is to be given to the people of Rogen. If something should happen to you before you reach Rogen, then Hakon the Black shall be the steersman."

Magnus looked into Hakon's face. "Eigil Haroldson comes of better family than I do, so do most of the other men; choose among them a leader."

Hakon grimaced, as if he had tasted something that was bitter. "A man shall be judged by his deeds, not by his father's or his grandfather's name. Eigil Haroldson is rash: brave with a sword but not wise in council. Erp the Traveler has told me that of those he has taught the meaning of the stars, you understand them best, and after you, Hakon the Black."

Magnus smiled. I saw that Hakon's words had pleased him. "If you have not returned by nightfall, we shall march for the hall; but what are your orders, once we get there? How shall we know if you are prisoners or slain?"

Hakon glanced at me, and bit his lip. I could see that he had no answer. "We have the word of the priests for our safety. What shield that is, we do not know. We have no choice but to trust them. I have chosen you to lead the men, not because you can follow an order, but because you can give one."

Magnus nodded; then he turned to me while he spoke to Hakon. "Take good care of Helga."

First Hakon frowned, but then he smiled before he answered. "When two men want the same gold ring, they let their swords decide the ownership. But love is not a golden ring, it is a gift that is given you and cannot be won by the sword."

Now Magnus the Fair, who among us was master of words, said nothing. He pressed Hakon's hand, looked at me for a moment, turned, and walked away.

I wanted to run after him, and say that I was sorry; instead I stood still, staring miserably at the ground.

Once more I saw Magnus the Fair that day. It was as we were leaving. The priests had loaned us horses to ride to the meeting with Hugues. As we rode from the buildings of Saint Meen, following the path that skirted the meadow, I saw Magnus standing alone, watching us. I waved to him, but he did not wave back.

26

THE PATH leading to Rark's hall was broad enough for us to ride in pairs. Rark and Father Christopher rode at the head of the group. Hakon, riding beside a priest with a pale face and an eagle's nose, followed. Then came Erp the Traveler, who rode a little ahead of the priest who accompanied him. I was last and had as companion the youngest of the priests, the Norseman Michel. In front of me rode Nils Haroldson and a fat priest with a sour face, who sat ill on a horse.

I looked at my companion. He gazed straight ahead. When I spoke to him he hardly answered. Remembering that it was he who had warned us about how many men were in Hugues' hall, I was surprised by his silence and seeming unfriendliness. I held my horse back, and let the others get a little farther ahead; then I turned and asked him, "Are you offering us to your god? Is it to our death that you are leading us?"

The priest turned pale at my words, and shook his head vigorously.

"Why then will you not speak with me?" I asked.

"Father Christopher hates the Norsemen, and good

are his reasons. But he has sworn for your safety by his god, and you can trust him."

My horse was eager to join its companions and started to trot, though I held the reins tight. "We have done no harm to the Franks," I said.

The priest looked at me. "You killed the servant."

We had caught up with the others again. "But he was a spy," I insisted.

"He was an old and foolish man," the priest replied.

Rark's hall — or Hugues' hall, for it was he who sat in the high seat — was the largest building we had yet seen in Frankland. The main hall was as big as the Church of Saint Meen; but the buildings which surrounded the church were low, while the stables and servants' quarters here were as imposing as many of the halls we had passed in our travels.

The buildings were placed next to each other in the form of a square, with a yard in the middle. Towards the fields there were no windows, only small openings in the walls through which arrows could be shot, should the hall be attacked. The entrance to the hall was open when we came. The two strong oak doors were pulled back. So wide and tall was the opening that two men on horseback could ride through, side by side. From the outside, the hall looked grim, and led one to think of battle and death; therefore, the friendliness of the yard in the middle surprised one. The main hall had six windows with glass to let in the light. The other buildings had many openings, which could be closed with wooden shutters to keep out the rain and wind.

Servants took our horses and led them to the stables. In the manure bed, in the corner of the yard nearest the stables, I saw many chickens scratching for food.

As soon as we had dismounted, we drew together in small groups: the priests in one, and we in another.

"It is the most beautiful hall I have ever seen," Hakon said. Nils Haroldson looked up at Rark, with a respect he had never shown him before.

Erp the Traveler glanced about nervously, and remarked, "I don't like the looks of the bear pit."

Three steps led to the door of the main hall. We walked towards them, following the priests. The door was opened by a man so finely dressed that I thought it must be Hugues, but it was merely his head servant.

Beyond the entrance was a small room. Again we had to climb stairs, and go through two more large doors; like the gates, these doors were open. We followed the priest up the stairs and stepped into a large room. As soon as we entered, the priests stepped aside, so that the first person we saw was Hugues.

At the end of the room, which was as large as Earl Hakon's hall, and much more splendid, stood a long table. Behind the table were beautifully carved chairs. Hugues sat in the center one, which was larger than the others.

I do not know why I expected his hair to be black. It was not; it was very long and fair like gold. It fell to his shoulders and curled on his black coat. The woman — Rark's wife . . . Hugues' wife — was dark. Her hair was black like the raven's wing. She sat at Hugues' side. When she saw Rark, her mouth opened and shut; then she looked away.

Hugues did not bid us welcome, merely looked at us with contempt in his eyes, while his hand played with a little dagger that had a golden handle. We felt not like guests, but like prisoners who were being brought before their captors. At first I thought that only Hugues and his wife were in the room, for no others were seated at the table. A sudden cough made me look away from Hugues' arrogant face and see whom else the hall held. Along the walls, on either side of us, stood ten armed men, with their hands on their swords' hilts.

"A strange welcome they give their guests here in Frankland," said Hakon loudly, and grabbed the hilt of his own sword.

"What says the barbarian?" Hugues asked, and looked at Rark.

"He says that since the Franks have lost their faith in the laws of their god, they have lost their manners, as well."

Hugues let the little dagger fall with a clatter upon the table; and for a moment, I thought that he was going to order all of us to be killed. But he smiled, picked up the dagger again, and spoke to Hakon. (Naturally, I had not understood what either Hugues or Rark had said, for they spoke in the Frank language; but later while we were eating, Michel told me what had passed between them.)

Now Hugues addressed Hakon, and his words were honeyed. Hakon looked at Rark. Rark, in turn, asked the Norse priest to tell us what our host had said. Michel stepped forward from the group of priests who stood at the entrance. I saw that he was frightened, and smiled to give him courage.

"He says it is a great honor to have so famous a Norseman visit him in his hall."

Hakon made a small bow and said, "A friend's hall is a Norseman's home."

I do not know whether Michel told what Hakon had said, but he must have changed the meaning that lay behind the words, for Hugues smiled as if he had been given a compliment.

Rark did not look at Hugues but only at his wife; she looked only at her hands, which lay folded in her lap. Hugues clapped his hands together; and I almost jumped, for I had been looking around the room, with my back towards him. The clapping of hands had been a signal for the servants. The well-dressed man who had stood at the entrance now came forward, and showed us to our places at the table.

Hugues had arranged us so that Hakon and Rark sat across from him and the woman whom both Rark and Hugues claimed as wife. The old priest, Father Christopher, sat between Rark and Hakon. On either side of them sat two men from Hugues' hird. Next to Hugues' men, who sat on Hakon's right, were Nils Haroldson and the fat priest who had been his companion on the ride to the hall. Beside them sat two more of Hugues' men; then Erp the Traveler and the priest who had accompanied him. On the left, beside those of Hugues' men who were nearest Rark, sat the priest with the nose like an eagle's beak; and at last, the priest whose name was Michel and myself.

I do not think that any of us had ever been served a better meal; certainly it was better fare than we received at Earl Hakon's table, yet we ate little. There were many kinds of meat, and they all were well cooked. Beside each plate was a little piece of cloth, to dry one's hands on. Hugues, himself, ate as cleanly as a cat. He did not use his fingers, but had a little fork, of the same shape as the very large ones we use on Rogen for turning hay. He would stick its two prongs into the meat, then cut with his knife as big a piece as he could eat, and lift it on the fork to his mouth.

Hakon asked Rark if that was the custom among the

Franks. Rark shook his head and said he had never seen it before. When Hugues noticed that Hakon was looking at his fork, he explained to Rark, "This is the custom among the people of Venice, who as everyone knows are even more refined than the people of Rome."

Seated next to Michel, I was more fortunate than the others, for each time that someone spoke in the Frank language, he whispered to me what had been said. Hakon, Erp, and Nils were now turned towards Rark, waiting for him to tell them what Hugues' remark had been. I could see that Rark had forgotten us. He was glaring at Hugues, and his voice trembled with anger when he spoke.

"Do they teach in that city, too, that man and wife are but words; and that a marriage blessed by God is as easily changed as the fashions of a vain woman?"

Hugues looked at his wife. Her face was pale, and the meat in front of her untouched. "Maria," Hugues began; but Rark interrupted him.

"Not Maria! That was the name of my wife. Her mother and father, being humble before their god, gave her that sainted name; but now surely, she must have another, for Maria was wed to Jacques de Bardinais. And since she was once wed to him, and he is alive, then she can be wed to no other!"

When Hugues did not reply, Rark turned to Father Christopher and shouted at him, "Have the laws of the Church changed? Are there new laws since I was last in Frankland?"

Father Christopher was staring at Hugues, as if he hoped he would answer for them both; but Hugues was looking at his wife. Finally, the priest said in a low tone, "The laws of the church have not changed. Marriage vows between two Christians only death can break; but if one of those who has been united under Christ should give up his god and worship idols, then he has broken the marriage vows, and is, as far as the Church is concerned, dead."

When Michel had finished telling me what the priest had said, I looked at him, trying to make his glance meet mine, for I had noticed that he was like Hakon, and could not tell lies so that one could believe them. The young priest turned away from me. "To worship idols is a sin," he whispered quickly, "the greatest sin a Christian can commit."

"But Rark has been faithful to his god!" I said aloud.

Suddenly Rark jumped up from his seat. Only half-way out of its leather scabbard did Rark draw his sword when I heard the sound of a bowstring being released. With a scream Rark fell forward, an arrow protruding from his back. For a moment none of us moved; surprise, not fear, lamed our limbs.

Slowly we turned our heads in the direction the arrow had come from. In front of the door to the hall stood five men with bow and arrow in hand, ready to shoot.

"It must be a mistake! It must be a mistake!" Michel muttered wildly.

I was looking at Hakon. He sat perfectly still, staring

at Hugues. I noticed that the muscles in his neck were twisted and I feared he would do what Hugues wished him to do: draw his sword so that the bowmen could shoot.

Only Rark's hands were moving, they kept clawing at the table, as if he wanted to crawl away. Suddenly the hands stopped and straightened themselves; then they were still. Slowly Rark slipped off the table. His body slid to the floor, but his head fell face upward in the lap of Father Christopher. The priest cried out, and jumped up from the bench. He made the Christian's sign, and then pointed at Hugues.

"He did not know. He did not know about it," Michel whispered to me; and I nodded, for I did not believe that the priests had wanted Rark's death.

Angrily Father Christopher was shouting at Hugues; but he kept looking at his wife with a strange smile on his face. She had not uttered a cry when Rark, the father of her children, had been slain. She had stared straight ahead. But now, in the middle of Father Christopher's angry outburst, she started to laugh. I shivered, for I had heard that laughter before. It was the laughter of Hjalte Gudbrandson: the laughter of those from whom the gods have taken their reason.

Hugues said something and two of his men carried the poor woman from the hall. I did not watch them. I felt certain that day and night, summer and winter had melted together for her, and would never part again.

When we could no longer hear the madwoman's laughter, Father Christopher turned to the young priest, Michel, and spoke a few words. Michel rose and walked over to Hakon.

"Father Christopher bade me tell you that he came here in good faith."

Hakon turned and looked at the old man a long time before he answered. "I have heard much of your god. He is a god of peace: this my friend Rark told me, when he lived among us in the north. Because of Rark I respected your god much. I see now that though you say you have only one god, you have many; for my friend's god could not be the same one as these men believe in."

Father Christopher looked intently at Hakon. He followed his words as if he understood them. When Father Michel told him what Hakon had said, he smiled a sad and forlorn smile.

Hugues had not risen from his place at the table; he was cleaning his nails with the little fork he had used for eating. The old priest said something to him, but he did not reply. Finally he turned to the Norse priest, Michel, and said something. Michel appeared very relieved.

"I am to tell you," he said to Hakon, "that you and your men are free to go. No harm will come to you if you leave your swords in your belts."

Hakon rose and looked at Hugues, as if he were about to speak to him; but then he determinedly looked away, and fell upon his knees beside Rark's lifeless body. Erp the Traveler, Nils Haroldson, and I stood up and made our way silently to where our dead friend

198

lay. Hakon looked up at us, then down again at Rark, before he spoke this verse:

> "All journeys end
> Break must the bow
> That the gods bend
> And the tides turn low."

He kissed the dead man on both cheeks, and walked from the hall without looking back. We followed him. Behind us we heard a man laugh: I believe it was Hugues.

When we came out into the light of the yard the sun blinded us, for the windows in the hall were not large and the room had been nearly in twilight.

Blinkingly, we looked about the yard. It was filled with armed men. Some of them were wounded. It took us a while to realize where those men had come from. When we guessed the truth, that they had come from the field of Saint Meen, a great and terrible anger rose within us. I looked at Hakon. He was as pale as the sand on the beach at night when a full moon shines on it. Nils, whose brother was in the camp in front of the abbey, was about to draw his sword; but Hakon with a word prevented him.

The priests had followed us out, and now they were looking about with expressions of astonishment which were not unlike our own. A man groaned; he was being held upright by his two companions. One of the priests ran over to him.

Hakon said to Michel, "Yours is a bloody god!"

The young priest shook his head; tears were forming in his eyes. Father Christopher shouted something. Soon servants brought out our horses. Hugues' men made place for us to mount. They looked sullen and angry; we could see in their faces that their victory had not been easily won.

When we sat on our horses, Hugues came out and spoke to Michel. The young priest looked at me pleadingly as he spoke to Hakon. "My parents were Norsemen. On my honor, we were innocent of this!"

Hakon looked down at the priest, then towards the portal, to make sure that the gates were open. "I believe you, but that is not what Hugues bade you tell me."

The priest lowered his head.

"Tell me what he said," Hakon insisted.

"He said that you are free to return to your land of ice; and there you are to tell that not all Franks are defenseless priests who can be robbed and slaughtered." Father Michel paused, swallowed, and turned his gaze to the ground; then he whispered, "He said that from now on, we will hang *all* the crows in the cherry trees."

"I shall tell in the north," Hakon replied, "that a coward's way is the same in all lands." Then he made his horse move closer to mine, and as he put his arm about my waist he whispered, "When you hear me shout, ride fast, and don't look back. Now walk your horse through the gate."

I nodded. Nils Haroldson and Erp the Traveler had already ridden ahead. I was about to follow them when

I heard Hakon's horse stamp. I looked back. His horse was rearing and acting as if it were trying to throw him. I stopped my horse, for I was surprised, knowing as I did that Hakon rode well. Hugues was laughing as Hakon's horse danced backward, shaking its head.

Then I saw the knife in Hakon's hand, and my own hand grabbed my belt; my dagger was gone. I dug my heels into the sides of my horse and let the rein loose. The frightened animal jumped and galloped through the open portal of the yard.

I heard a cry behind me and reined back my horse. Before I turned my head, I heard Hakon's scream, "Ride, Helga! Ride!"

"Hakon! Hakon!" I cried as I kicked my horse; but because of my fear I held the reins tight, and the horse danced.

"Let the reins go!" Hakon was beside me, he leaned over and tore the reins from my hands. As soon as the horse felt the bit loosen in its mouth, it started to gallop. I leaned forward and the wind whipped the mane in my face, while my ears heard the sound of hoofs striking the ground.

27

SWIFTER THAN ANY OF US had ever ridden before did our horses carry us back from Hugues' feast. We did not stop before the forest fell away, and we saw the Church of Saint Meen, the fields, and our camp. Then, as if we had made a spoken agreement, we all reined back our horses. They were wet with sweat and foaming at the mouth.

The landscape was completely still. The winds were asleep, as if time had deserted the earth, and the sun, which was low in the west, would not set but remain hanging there forever.

Slowly we rode our horses across the fields. We did not dare to look at each other for fear our courage would leave us. We tied our horses by the shed, then walked around counting the dead.

When Nils Haroldson came to his brother Eigil's body, he sat down on the ground and cried in the hopeless manner of a little child.

I was looking for Magnus the Fair. At first I could not find him; and hope sang within me, until I came to the north wall of the shed. He was not alone. Death had been kinder to Rigmor Ragnvaldsdaughter than life had been. She was sitting down, leaning against the wall, a gaping wound in her shoulder. Magnus lay in her lap, two arrows sticking from his body. I leaned over Rigmor and touched her face, for I thought for a moment that she was still alive. "No one shall come between you and your love ever again," I whispered.

"They are all here, and none can answer to his name," I heard Hakon say.

I ran to my horse and buried my head against its warm, living skin, for I could bear no longer looking at death's face.

"Helga!" Hakon's face was white and little beads of sweat covered his forehead. I looked at him but said nothing, and he only repeated my name. Then I started to cry, and Hakon embraced me and held me. I cried not only for the dead, but for the meaninglessness of what had happened.

Although I was crying, I could hear the clatter of a horse galloping from afar; and so strong is the instinct of life that I could not help looking up.

It was the Norse priest, Michel. He had been riding as hard as he could whip his horse forward. When he finally managed to bring his poor shaking horse to a halt, the priest was so out of breath that he could hardly speak to us.

"They are coming," he stammered. With horror he looked down at the dead man, who was lying near his horse's feet. It was Orm the Storyteller.

"Have you fresh horses at the Abbey?" Hakon asked, and pushed me in the direction of my horse. The priest nodded and Hakon called loudly the names of Erp and Nils, while he mounted his own horse.

I untied my horse. The poor beast looked at me as if it were trying to say, "I cannot carry you any farther." I jumped on its back, leaned over and stroked its neck, then trotted after Michel and Hakon towards the church.

Nils Haroldson would not leave the body of his brother. Erp had to force him back on his horse.

The young priest made certain that we were given the best horses that were left in the stables. While the servants changed our saddles, he told us what had happened at the hall after Hakon had thrown the knife at Hugues.

The knife had entered Hugues' shoulder, but it had not killed him, and he had ordered his men to pursue us. Father Christopher had stopped the men and argued with Hugues, saying that he must keep his promise to let us go in peace. The young Norse priest had not waited for the argument's outcome; fearing that Hugues' will would eventually be obeyed by his men, Father Michel had at once come to warn us. So hasty had been his departure that he had not even bothered to saddle his horse.

Hakon thanked the young priest; yet I could see by his expression that he did not believe that the other priests were innocent of the plot which had destroyed us. When the horses were ready and we were mounted, Father Michel came to me and said, "Your chief does not trust me."

"It is not you he does not trust," I said. "But we were twenty-four men and three women when we set out from Saint Malo. Now we are only four!"

Father Michel looked up at me, and his voice trembled when he spoke. "My god is a god of peace!"

I looked away when I answered. "Gods of peace will matter little so long as men worship the sword."

The priest, who had been holding my bridle, let go of it. The others were already riding ahead. I looked down and said farewell. Father Michel's head was bent; he was gazing at the ground.

"I shall have your friends buried," he whispered.

I kicked the side of my horse. Then I held it back, for I felt sorry for the priest. He had spoken the truth: his god — Father Michel's god, like Rark's god — was a god of peace. "Bury the man whose head is lying in the woman's lap in the same grave that you prepare for her," I said.

The priest nodded. I heard Hakon calling me. "Pray for them to your god!" I cried and dug my heels into the side of my horse and loosened the reins.

Hakon, Nils, and Erp had ridden back to the camp. When I came, they were dismounted; but Hakon ordered me not to get off my horse. He gave me a bow and some arrows. I looked at the bow: it had belonged to Magnus the Fair. Nils wanted to take a shield, but Hakon told him that it would only be in the way when he was riding.

At the same time that we wanted nothing more than to leave it, the field of Saint Meen held us as prisoners. Not before we heard in the distance the galloping of horses did Hakon give the signal for departure. When we came to the beginning of the forest, where the path to Dinan commences, we stopped to look back on that field which our eyes would never see again, but which our minds would visit often, until that time would come when we, too, would sleep without dreams.

Far behind us, we saw our pursuers. There were only ten men, and their horses were already tired. Hakon waved his hand as if he were saying farewell to someone, turned his horse, and trotted off into the forest. I faced my horse in the direction that Hakon had taken. Erp the Traveler passed me. Nils Haroldson and I turned in our saddles.

"Magnus!" I wanted to say; but my lips could not form the name. Mutely, I looked back at the field. The bells of the Church of Saint Meen started to ring. I glanced at Nils Haroldson. He smiled, though his cheeks were streaked with tears. I nodded and kicked my horse into a gallop.

28

WE RODE all night, stopping only a few times to give the horses a rest, and wipe their sweat-covered coats. Even when we rested, we dared not let the horses stand still, so we walked them slowly along the road. By morning we were near Dinan.

At a very small farm, Hakon bought bread and milk. Hakon had believed, to the very last, that he could buy Hugues with gold. This was our good fortune, for he had taken with him all of the gold he owned, in two leather bags tied around his waist, when we had visited Rark's hall. Had he left his gold behind with Magnus the Fair, then we should not have been able to buy bread now, for Hugues' men had robbed our dead comrades after they had killed them.

"The moon wanes, but grows full again; so it is with Hakon's luck," said Erp the Traveler while we ate our morning meal.

I glanced at Nils Haroldson, whose brother lay in the field of Saint Meen, and I said to myself, "If Erp's daughter had not been left behind with those who guarded *Munin*, Erp would not have said those words."

"To have faith in one's luck is to be led by a shadow," said Hakon.

Nils Haroldson cursed the gods; then he said, "When we are back on Rogen, then I shall talk of luck having returned."

When we could see the walls of Dinan we left the road and took a smaller path, for we feared the Franks would kill us, now that we were only four. By noon we reached the fjord. We rested at the same place where we had camped before. Weary though we were, we did not dare to sleep.

Our hearts rejoiced at the sight of the water; it was the road home. We bathed. For the first time on our journey back to Saint Malo, we laughed. As we swam, life came back to us; and death, as a star of night that fades in morning, disappeared. When we were dressed again, the thought of yesterday returned. When I saw the charred wood, from the fire we had built when we were here last, I wept. I wanted to leave at once; but Hakon said our horses were too tired, and we would have to wait until late afternoon.

"Helga?"

With the end of a burned stick, I was drawing lines on the calf of one of my legs. "Yes," I answered; but I kept on decorating my skin, and did not look up at Hakon, who had sat down beside me.

"I feel so old."

I knew what Hakon meant, for I too felt old; not grown up, but old like Freya on Rogen.

"Do you think we shall ever be as we were before?"

I glanced at Hakon. He was looking down at his hands, which he kept knotting and unknotting. "No," I said, "not as we have been before, but neither as we are now. Of a wound, you either live or die. If you live, then the wound heals though the scar remains."

Hakon touched one of my hands. I looked up at him; and I saw that his face was like an old man's.

"Will you be my wife?"

I turned away; not because I did not know what answer I wanted to give, but because I thought of Magnus and I knew that the winds of tomorrow were beginning to blow. I felt ashamed of my sudden happiness.

"Are you thinking of your birth?"

I wrinkled my brow, for I did not know what Hakon meant. Then when I understood, I sighed and smiled. Truly, I was not a slave any more, for I had not even thought of it.

"I will marry you, Hakon."

At my words a smile broke timidly forth on Hakon's face. He put his hands on my shoulders and leaned my head on his chest. "Once I thought the gods' only message to us was that we had to live; now I think their message is that we must grow wise enough to love." Hakon untied the leather string, on which was hung the silver Thor's hammer that he wore around his neck; and as is the custom among the Norsemen, Hakon threw the tiny hammer into my lap.

We left our old camp near Dinan as the sun set. We rode all night. In the morning, when the sun was but a hand's breadth above that line in the east where the sky meets the earth, we were back on the island with our friends. All was well there. No harm had come to any of them, nor to *Munin*. The sight of our ship comforted us, as our first view of the water had done.

Hakon had to tell all that had happened to us. I could not bear to listen, for Hakon's sparse words pained me, yet I could not have told the story differently.

I walked down to the ship, and lay down in the sand beside it. Although I had thought that sleep would never come to me again, it came silently and closed my eyes.

In the world of sleep neither death nor age exists. In my dream that morning, I was a child again, and Hakon's father, Olaf Sigurdson, had placed me on his knee. Suddenly Father Olaf's face changed and became the face of Magnus the Fair. He looked at me with such wonderful sadness that I could not bear to look back at him. In my dream, I closed my eyes. When I opened them again, I was no longer a child. I was my own age, and I was sitting alone in the grass on the field of Saint Meen. I was braiding flowers into a chain, as I had done so often in springtime on Rogen, when the island is covered with flowers. While I was weaving the stems of the flowers, I was crying; but I did not know why.

Someone shook me. I awoke. It was Hakon, who had come to tell me that the midday meal was prepared. I looked up at him unhappily, for it is not pleasant to be awakened from a dream, even if it is a very sad one.

"Helga, Helga, you must not cry any more!"

I put my hands to my face and felt my moist cheeks. "It was a dream," I said.

211

By late afternoon, the tide was high. We decided to put *Munin* in the water again, and anchor her out where it was deep. Being so few, we felt safer sleeping on board the ship. We had great difficulty getting the ship back into the water. We used the trunks of small trees as rollers, but it took all our strength and much time to do it.

We were all very tired; and at sunset, we went on board *Munin*, intending to sleep. But just as the last rays of the parting sun had left the sky, the guard called out that he had sighted a small boat coming towards us. It was rowed by three men, each handling two oars; in its stern sat a fourth man. The boat was heavily loaded, for it lay low in the water. When it came near to us, we could see that the man in the stern was a priest.

One of the rowers hailed us in our own language. Hakon ordered the boat to pull alongside *Munin*, midship. When it bumped against our side, we saw that our guest was Rark's uncle, the high priest of Saint Malo.

With great difficulty, the old man got on board our ship. As he stepped over the railing, he made with his fingers the Christian's sign. He waved his hand; and that member of the small boat's crew who had spoken in the Norse language came on board *Munin*. He was a short, but strong-looking young man, with a red beard.

The old priest looked about the ship. He seemed to be counting how many of us there were; then he said something to the oarsman in the Frank language.

The young man turned to Hakon. "Father Claude has heard with sorrow the news from Saint Meen. He wishes to thank you for your friendship to his nephew."

Erp the Traveler whispered loudly, "No man rows out at night on the fjord if he only wishes to look at the moon."

The priest's servant told him what Erp had said. For a moment, the priest was silent as he looked out over the water. When he spoke to his servant, his voice was low and he spoke long.

The young man pulled at his red beard and glanced at Erp before he told us the priest's words. "It is true that an old man does not endanger his health by seeking the damp winds of night unless his honor bids him do it. As for the moon, it is long since I found pleasure in walking by its light." The oarsman shifted his gaze to Hakon, then he continued, "I have come to warn you that you had better sail when the next high tide is here, for three of Hugues' men are in Saint Malo. They tell everyone that you have much gold and that you are defenseless."

Hakon looked hard at the priest. I could see that he was trying to find out if the old man was in earnest, or was merely trying to get rid of unwelcome guests. "No man is defenseless," Hakon said slowly, "as long as his sword hangs at his side."

When the red-bearded servant told the priest what Hakon had said, the old man made an impatient movement with his arm, and spoke almost angrily, "Through the taverns of the town, the words are running of your wealth, and each time the tale is told, your riches grow."

Hakon looked up at the sky. There was little wind; but what there was, was favorable for us. "I thank you for your warning, but we have few supplies on board." He stopped and gazed thoughtfully at the old priest. "Yet better a hungry stomach than a still heart. We shall sail when the tide is high."

The priest smiled when the servant had told him what Hakon had said. He gave an order to the men who were seated in the small boat, and then spoke again to the red-bearded man.

The servant bowed first towards the priest and then towards Hakon. "My master has brought food and wine for your journey. He hopes that you will not think him too ungenerous, for he had little time to gather what he has brought." Before Hakon could thank him, the old priest said something else for the servant to tell us. "Father Claude bids me say that he is giving you these gifts as a Frank, and because his family owes you a debt of honor, not as a priest of his god, for between his god and those who worship false gods, no peace can exist."

Hakon looked at me before he answered. "In my own country, far to the north, there lives a man with grizzly hair and beard. He is called Hakon, Earl of Tronhjem. He, too, thinks so little of the power of his gods that he needs to fight their battles for them. Many priests of the new god has he killed for the glory of Odin. I think he has brought on our gods more shame than glory. I think it would be far better if man took the bloody sword and called it his own; and to the gods gave the honor of those deeds done from love and the pitying heart."

When the old priest had been told Hakon's words, he rose and placed his right hand on Hakon's shoulder. He spoke very solemnly. His face was a little sad, as a man's face often is when he speaks of things that he has only dared to think about when he was alone. While the red-bearded servant told us the priest's words, the old man himself moved away from us, closer to the railing, and bowed his head.

"Much wisdom you have for one so young. I foresee that soon we shall worship the same god. I do not know if I do wrong — if I do, I pray God will forgive me, for His servant has grown old — but I give you the blessing of Christ. And I shall pray that you return safely to your own land." The old priest covered his face with his hands, for man will ever question love.

The priest's hand had been generous when he selected from his storehouses and his cellar. When we loaded the supplies, we realized that we had enough on board for the long journey to Tronhjem.

The priest bade us farewell. As a parting gift, he gave Hakon a small metal cross. The moon was up. We watched the priest's boat disappear. The tide was almost slack. Soon we, too, should sail.

EPILOGUE

THE SLAVE'S TALE is over; now begins another story, which there is no need to tell, for sorrow fits our tongues, and happy tales make us move uncomfortably on the bench. Maybe some day, tales of love and adventure need not end unhappily to tell our hearts that they are true.

We traveled over an autumn sea, resting one night on that Frank island where we had camped when we were so many, and our memories were so young: that island that we had called "Hakon's Luck." We suffered much, for the winds are hard masters in the north when summer has passed; but to Tronhjem we came, with torn sail and broken steering oar.

Earl Hakon was dead, slain by his slave Kark; and Olaf Trygveson was ruler of all of Norway. Earl Hakon's statues to the old gods had been burned, and in Tronhjem we heard the bells of the new god, as we had heard them in Saint Meen and Saint Malo.

Not long did we stay in Tronhjem, for our eyes longed to see Rogen. With new sail and steering oar, we set sail from Tronhjem, and the weather took pity on us and blew us gently home.

All that happened long ago; and now I am wife of

Hakon the Lucky and am called Helga of Rogen. But when the winds in summer breathe gently on our island, then memories come back of the lands far to the south, where the sun now kisses warmly the earth that covers Magnus, Rark, Eigil Haroldson, Rigmor Ragnvaldsdaughter, Freya the Young, and all the others who sailed with us.

The old gods are gone. In Odin's clearing stands a house to Rark's god, who is called Jesus Christ. Odin and Thor are only names now; names that we use to frighten the children into behaving. The god of the south is now the god of the north, as well.